Gough Hotel
Cumberland.

8.7.

= A. 6. $\frac{1918}{2}$

·AGG100/2

OBSERVATIONS,

RELATIVE CHIEFLY TO

PICTURESQUE BEAUTY,

Made in the YEAR 1772,

On several PARTS of ENGLAND;

PARTICULARLY THE

MOUNTAINS, AND LAKES

OF

Cumberland, and Westmoreland.

THIRD EDITION.

VOL. II.

By WILLIAM GILPIN, M. A.

PREBENDARY OF SALISBURY;

AND

VICAR OF BOLDRE, IN NEW FOREST, NEAR LYMINGTON.

London;

PRINTED FOR R. BLAMIRE, STRAND.

1792.

OBSERVATIONS

ON

Several PARTS of ENGLAND,

ESPECIALLY

The LAKES, &c.

SECTION XVI.

HAVING refreſhed ourſelves, and our horſes, after a fatiguing morning, we proceeded along the vale of Buter‐mer; and following the courſe of the river, as far as the inequalities of the ground would admit, we ſoon came to another lake, ſtill more beautiful, than that we had left above. The two lakes bear a great reſemblance to each other. Both are oblong: both wind

round promontories; and both are furrounded
by mountains. But the lower lake is near a
mile longer, than the upper one; the lines it
forms are much eafier; and tho it has lefs
wood on it's banks, the lofs is compenfated
by a richer difplay of rocky fcenery. The
forms of thefe rocks are in general, beautiful;
moft of them being broken into grand fquare
furfaces. This fpecies, as we have already
obferved,* are in a greater ftyle, than the
cragg, which is fhattered into more diminutive parts.

With this rocky fcenery much hilly ground
is intermixed. Patches of meadow alfo, here
and there, on the banks of the lake, improve
the variety. Nothing is wanting but a little
more wood, to make this lake, and the vale
in which it lies, a very inchanting fcene; or
rather a fucceffion of inchanting fcenes; for
the hills, and rifing grounds, into which it
every where fwells, acting in due fubordina-
tion to the grand mountains, which inviron
the whole vale, break and feparate the area
of it into fmaller parts. Many of thefe form

---

* See Vol. I. page 108.

little

little vallies, and other receffes, which are very picturefque.

: Not far from this lake the mountain of Grafmer appears rifing above all the mountains in it's neighbourhood. A *lake* of this name we had already feen in our road between Amblefide, and Kefwick; but there is no connection between the *lake*, and the *mountain*.

This mountain forms rather a vaft ridge, than a pointed fummit; and is connected with two or three other mountains of inferior dignity: itfelf is faid to be equal to Skiddaw; which is the common gage of altitude through the whole country; and therefore it may be fuppofed to be the higheft. No mountain afpires to be higher than Skiddaw: fome boaft an equal height: but two or three only have real pretenfions.

Grafmer, and the mountains in it's neighbourhood, from the eaftern boundary of the vale, which we now traverfed; a vale at leaft five miles in length, and one third of that fpace in breadth. Our road carried us near

the

the village of Brackenthwait, which lies at
the bottom of Grafmer.

Here we had an account of an inundation
occafioned by the burfting of a water-fpout.
The particulars, which are well authenticated,
are curious.—In that part, where Grafmer is
connected with the other high lands in it's
neighbourhood, three little ftreams take their
origin; of which the Liffa is the leaft inconfiderable. The courfe of this ftream down
the mountain is very fteep, and about a mile
in length. It's bed, and the fides of the
mountain all around, are profufely fcattered
with loofe ftones, and gravel. On leaving
the mountain, the Liffa divides the vale,
through which we now paffed; and, after a
courfe of four or five miles, falls into the
Cocker.

On the 9th of September 1760, about midnight, the water-fpout fell upon Grafmer,
nearly, as was conjectured, where the three
little ftreams, juft mentioned, iffue from their
fountains.

At

At firſt it ſwept the whole ſide of the mountain, and charging itſelf with all the rubbiſh
it found there, made it's way into the vale,
following chiefly the direction of the Liſſa.
At the foot of the mountain it was received
by a piece of arable ground; on which it's
violence firſt broke. Here it tore away trees,
ſoil, and gravel; and laid all bare, many feet
in depth, to the naked rock. Over the next
ten acres it ſeems to have made an immenſe
roll; covering them with ſo vaſt a bed of
ſtones; that no human art can ever again
reſtore the ſoil.

When we ſaw the place, tho twelve years
after the event, many marks remained, ſtill
flagrant, of this ſcene of ruin. We ſaw the
natural bed of the Liſſa, a mere contracted
rivulet; and on it's banks the veſtiges of a
ſtony channel, ſpreading far and wide, almoſt
enough to contain the waters of the Rhine,
or the Danube. It was computed from the
flood-marks, that in many parts the ſtream
muſt have been five or ſix yards deep; and
near a hundred broad; and if it's great velo-
city be added to this weight of water, it's
force will be found equal to almoſt any
effect.

On

On the banks of this ftony channel, we faw a few fcattered houfes, a part of the village of Brackenthwait, which had a wonderful efcape. They ftood at the bottom of Grafmer, rather on a rifing ground; and the current, taking it's firft direction towards them, would have undermined them in a few moments, (for the foil was inftantly laid bare) had not a projection of native rock, the interior ftratum, on which the houfes had unknowingly been founded, refifted the current, and given it a new direction. Unlefs this had intervened, it is probable, the houfes, and all their inhabitants (fo inftantaneous was the ruin) had been fwept away together.

In paffing farther along the vale, we faw other marks of the fury of this inundation; bridges had been thrown down, houfes carried off, and woods rooted up. But it's effects on a ftone-caufeway were thought the moft furprizing. This fabric was of great thicknefs; and fupported on each fide by an enormous bank of earth. The memory of man could trace it, unaltered in any particular, near a hundred years: but by the foundnefs and firmnefs of it's parts and texture, it feemed

as

as if it had stood for ages. It was almost a
doubt, whether it were a work of nature, or
of art. This maffy mole the deluge not only
carried off; but, as if it turned it into fport,
made it's very foundations the channel of it's
own stream.

Having done all this mifchief, not only
here, but in many other parts, the Liffa
threw all it's waters into the Cocker, where
an end was put to it's devaftation : for tho
the Cocker was unable to contain fo immenfe
an increafe; yet as it flows through a more
level country, the deluge fpread far and wide,
and wafted it's ftrength in one vaft, ftagnant
inundation.

Having paffed through the vale of Butermer, we entered another beautiful fcene, the
vale of Lorton.

This vale, like all the paft, prefents us
with a landfcape, intirely new. No lakes, no
rocks are here, to blend the ideas of dignity,
and grandeur with that of beauty. All is
fimplicity, and repofe. Nature, in this fcene,
lays totally afide her majeftic frown, and wears
only a lovely fmile.

B 4   The

The vale of Lorton is of the extended kind, running a confiderable way between mountains, which range at about a mile's diftance. They are near enough to fkreen it from the ftorm; and yet not fo impending as to exclude the fun. Their fides, tho not fmooth, are not much diverfified. A few knolls and hollows juft give a little variety to the broad lights and fhades, which over-fpread them.

This vale, which enjoys a rich foil, is in general a rural, cultivated fcene; tho in many parts the ground is beautifully broken, and abrupt. A bright ftream, which might almoft take the name of a river, pours along a rocky channel; and fparkles down number-lefs little cafcades. It's banks are adorned with wood; and varied with different objects; a bridge; a mill; a hamlet; a glade over-hung with wood; or fome little fweet recefs; or natural vifta, through which the eye ranges, between irregular trees, along the windings of the ftream.

Except the mountains, nothing in all this fcenery is *great*; but every part is filled with thofe fweet engaging paffages of nature, which

tend

tend to footh the mind, and inftill tranquillity.

————The paſſions to divine repoſe
Perſuaded yield; and love and joy alone
Are waking: love and joy, ſuch as await
An angel's meditation————

Scenes of this kind, (however pleaſing) in
which few objects occur, either of *grandeur*
or *peculiarity*, in a ſingular manner elude
the powers of verbal deſcription. They almoſt elude the power of colours. The ſoft
and elegant form of beauty is hard to hit:
while the ſtrong, harſh feature is a mark,
which every pencil can ſtrike.

But tho a *peculiar* difficulty attends the
verbal deſcription of theſe mild and quiet
haunts of Nature; yet undoubtedly *all* her
ſcenery is ill-attempted in language.

Mountains, rocks, broken ground, water,
and wood, are the ſimple materials, which
ſhe employs in all her beautiful pictures:
but the variety and harmony, with which
ſhe employs them are infinite. In deſcription
theſe words ſtand only for *general ideas*:
on her charts each is *detailed* into a thouſand
varied

varied forms. Words may give the great
outlines of a country. They can meafure the
dimenfions of a lake. They can hang it's
fides with wood. They can rear a caftle
on fome projecting rock: or place an ifland
near this, or the other fhore. But their range
extends no farther. They cannot mark the
characteriftic diftinctions of each fcene—
the touches of nature—her living tints—her
endlefs varieties, both in form and colour,
——In a word, all her elegant *peculiarities*
are beyond their reach. Language is equally
unable to convey thefe to the eye; as the
eye is to convey the various divifions of found
to the ear,

The pencil, it is true, offers a more perfect mode of defcription. It fpeaks a language
more intelligible; and defcribes the fcene in
ftronger, and more varied terms. The fhapes,
and hues of objects it delineates, and marks,
with more exactnefs. It gives the lake the
louring fhade of tempeft; or the glowing
blufh of fun-fet. It fpreads a warmer, or a
colder tint on the tufts of the foreft. It adds
form to the caftle; and tips it's fhattered
battlements with light.—But all this, all that
words can exprefs, or even the pencil defcribe,

are

are grofs, infipid fubſtitutes of the living
ſcene.* We may be pleafed with the deſcription, and the picture: but the foul can
feel neither, unleſs the force of our own
imagination aid the poet's, or the painter's
art; exalt the idea; and *picture things unſeen.*

Hence it perhaps follows, that the perfection of the art of painting is not ſo much
attained by an endeavour to form an exact
refemblance of nature in a *nice reprefentation of*
all her minute parts, which we confider as
almoft impracticable, ending generally in flat-
nefs, and infipidity; as by aiming to give
thofe bold, thofe ftrong characteriftic touches
which excite the imagination; and lead it to
form half the picture itfelf. Painting is the
art of deceiving; and it's great perfection lies
in the exercife of this art.

Hence it is that genius, and an accurate knowledge of nature are as requifite in examining a

---

* This is not at all inconfiftent with what is faid in the
119th page. *Here* we fpeak chiefly of the *detail* of nature's
works: *there* of the *compofition.* The nearer we approach the
character of nature in every mode of imitation, no doubt the
better: yet ftill there are many irregularities and deformities
in the natural fcene, which we may wifh to correct—that is,
to correct, by improving one part of nature by another.

picture,

picture, as in painting one. The cold, untu-
tored eye, tho it may enjoy the *real* scene, (be
it history,* landscape, or what it will) is unmoved at the best *representation*. It does not
see an *exact* resemblance of what it sees abroad ;
and having no *internal pencil*, if I may so speak,
to work within; it is utterly unable to *ad-
minister* a picture to itself. Whereas the
learned eye,† versed equally in nature, and
art,

---

* History-painting is certainly the most elevated species.
Nothing exalts the human mind so much, as to see the great
actions of our fellow-creatures brought before the eye. But
this pleasure we seldom find in painting. So much is required from the history-painter, so intimate a knowledge both of
nature and art, that we rarely see a history-piece, even from
the best masters, that is able to *raise raptures*. We may admire the colouring, or the execution; or some under-part;
but the *soul is seldom reached*. The imagination soars beyond
the picture.——In the inferior walks of painting, where less
is required, more of course is performed: and tho we
have few good pictures in history, we have many in portrait,
in landscape, in animal-life, dead-game, fruit, and flowers.
History painting is a mode of epic; and tho the literary
world abounds with admirable productions in the lower walks
of poetry, an epic is the wonder of an age.

† The admirers of painting may be divided into two
classes:——The inferior admirer values himself on *distin-
guishing the master*—on knowing the peculiar touch of each
pencil;

art, eafily compares the picture with it's
archetype : and when it finds the characteriftic
touches of nature, the imagination immediately
takes fire; and glows with a thoufand beau‐
tiful ideas, *fuggefted* only by the canvas.
When the canvas therefore is fo artificially
wrought, as to fuggeft thefe ideas in the
ftrongeft manner, the picture is then moft
perfect. This is generally beft done by little

---

pencil; and the ruling tint of every pallet. But he has no
feeling. If the picture be an *original*, or if it be in the
mafter's *beft manner* (which may be the cafe of many a bad
picture) it is the object of his veneration; tho the ftory be
ill-told, the characters feebly marked, and a total deficiency
appear in every excellence of the art.

The more liberal profeffor, (and who alone is here confider‐
ed as capable of *adminiftering* a picture to himfelf) thinks the
knowledge of names, (any farther than as it marks excellence,
till we get a better criterion,) is the bane of the art he ad‐
mires. A work, worthy of admiration, may be produced by
an inferior hand; and a paltry compofition may efcape from
a mafter. He would have the *intrinfic merit* of a work, not
any *arbitrary ftamp* proclaim it's excellence. In examining
a picture, he leaves the *name* intirely out of the queftion. It
may miflead, it cannot affift, his judgment. The characters
of nature, and the knowledge of art, are all he looks for:
the reft, be they Michael Angelo's, or Raphael's, he defpifes
as the bubbles of picture-dealers; the mere fweepings, and
refufe of Italian garrets.

labour;

labour, and great knowledge. It is knowledge only, which infpires that free, that fearlefs, and determined pencil, fo expreffive in a fkilful hand. As to the *minutiæ* of nature, the picturefque eye will generally fuggeft them better itfelf; and yet give the artift, as he deferves, the credit of the whole.

We fometimes indeed fee pictures *highly finifhed*, and *yet full of fpirit*. They will bear a nice examination at hand, and yet lofe nothing of their diftant effect. But fuch pictures are fo exceedingly rare, that I fhould think, few painters would in prudence attempt a *laboured manner*. Indeed, as pictures are not defigned to be feen through a microfcope, but at a proper diftance, it is labour thrown away.*

Hence it is that even a rough fketch, by the hand of a mafter, will often ftrike the imagination beyond the moft finifhed work.

---

* In the higher walks of painting I know of no artift, who does not lofe his fpirit in attempting to finifh highly. In the inferior walks we have a few. Among the firft we may rank Van Huyfum, who painted flowers, and fruits, with equal labour and fpirit. And yet even here, I own I have more pleafure in helping myfelf to thefe delicacies from the bolder works of Baptifte.

I have

I have feen the learned eye pafs unmoved
along rows of pictures by the cold, and inanimate pencil of fuch a mafter as Carlo Marat;
and ftart aftonifhed, when it came to a fketch
of Rubens. In one cafe the painter endea-
vouring in vain to *adminifter every thing* by
giving the full roundnefs, and fmoothnefs to
every part, inftead of the bold, characteriftic
touches of nature, had *done too much :* in
the other, tho the work was left unfinifhed,
yet many of the bold *characteriftic touches*
being thrown in, enough was done to excite
the imagination of the fpectator, which could
eafily *fupply the reft*.

A very ingenious writer * indeed gives another reafon for our being better pleafed with
a fketch, than with a finifhed piece. *The
imagination,* fays he, *is entertained with the
promife of fomething more; and does not ac-
quiefce in the prefent object of the fenfe*. But
this obfervation, I think, is fcarce founded on
truth. It is true *the imagination does not ac-
quiefce in the prefent object of the fenfe :* but;
I fhould fuppofe, not becaufe it is entertained

---

* Burke on the fublime and beautiful, Part II. Sect. XI.

with a *promise of something more*; but becaufe
it has the power, of *creating something more
itself.* If *a promise of something more,* were
the caufe of this pleafure, it fhould feem, that
a fketch, in it's rudeft form, would be more
pleafing, than when it is more advanced: for
the imagination muft have ftill *higher* entertainment in proportion to the *largenefs* of the
promife. But this is not the cafe. The
fketch, in it's naked chalk-lines, affects us
little in comparifon. The inftrument muft
be tuned higher, to excite vibrations in the
imagination.

Again, on the fame fuppofition, one fhould
imagine, that the rude beginning, or rough
plan of a houfe, would pleafe us more than the
compleat pile; for *the imagination is entertained with the promife of fomething more.*
But, I believe, no one was ever fo well pleafed
with an unfinifhed fhell, amidft all it's rubbifh
of fcaffolding, paper-windows, and other deformities; as with a ftructure compleat in all
it's members, and fet off with all it's proper
decorations.—But on the fnppofition I have
ventured to fuggeft, we fee why the *fketch* may
pleafe beyond the *picture*; tho the *unfinifhed
fabric* difappoints. An elegant houfe is a
compleat

compleat object. The imagination can rife no higher. It receives full fatisfaction. But a picture is *not an object itfelf*; but only the *reprefentation* of an object. We may eafily therefore conceive, that it may fall below it's archetype; and alfo below the imagination of the fpectator, whofe fancy may be more picturefque, than the hand of the artift, who compofed the picture. In this cafe, a fketch may afford the fpectator more pleafure, as it gives his imagination freer fcope; and fuffers it to compleat the artift's imperfect draught from the fund of it's own richer, and more perfect ideas.

The variety of fcenes, which nature exhibits; and their infinite combinations, and peculiarities, to which neither language, nor colours, unaided by imagination, can, in any degree, do juftice; gave occafion to thefe remarks, which have carried me perhaps too far into digreffion.

We had to regret, that we faw the vale of Lorton only in half it's beauty. It was at too late an hour; and the evening befides was dark. The morning had been cloudy;

in

in some part of it rather tempestuous; and we thought ourselves then very happy in the disposition of the weather; for as we had before seen the mountains in a clear atmosphere; it was a desirable variety to see the grand effects they produced in a storm. A mountain is an object of grandeur; and it's dignity receives new force by mixing with the clouds; and arraying itself in the majesty of darkness. Here the idea of *infinity* * produces strongly the sublime. But the chearful scenes of such a vale as this, pretend not to dignity: they are mere scenes of tranquillity. The early ray of dawn, the noon-tide shade, or evening-glow, are the circumstances, in which they most rejoice: a storm, in any shape, will injure them. Here therefore we might have dispensed with more light, and sunshine. Or at the close of the day we might have wished for a quiet, tranquil hour, when the glimmering surfaces of things are sometimes perhaps more pleasing—at all times certainly more soothing, than images of the brightest hue:

---

* See page 228. Vol. I.

When through the duſk obſcurely ſeen
Sweet evening-objeᢏs intervene.

The evening, which grew more tempeſtu-
ous, began to cloſe upon us, as we left the
more beautiful parts of the vale of Lorton.
We were ſtill about ſix miles from Keſwick;
and had before us a very wild country, which
probably would have afforded no great amuſement even in full day: but amid the obſcurity,
which now overſpread the landſcape, the imagination was left at large; and painted many
images, which perhaps did not really exiſt,
upon the dead colouring of nature. Every
great and pleaſing form, whether clear, or
obſcure, which we had ſeen during the day,
now played, in ſtrong imagery before the
fancy: as when the grand chorus ceaſes, ideal
muſic vibrates in the ear.

In one part, a view pleaſed us much; tho
perhaps, in ſtronger light, it might have
eſcaped notice. The road made a ſudden
dip into a little, winding valley; which being
too abrupt for a carriage, was eaſed by a

C 2   bridge:

bridge: and the form of the arch was what we commonly find in Roman aqueducts. At least such it appeared to us. The winding road; the woody valley, and broken ground below; the mountain beyond; the form of the bridge, which gave a classic air to the scene; and the obscurity, which melted the whole into one harmonious mass; made all together a very pleasing view.

But it soon grew too dark even for the imagination to roam. It was now ten o'clock; and tho in this northern climate, the twilight of a clear summer-evening affords, even at that late hour, a bright effulgence; yet now all was dark.

> ————————————A faint, erroneous ray
> Glanced from th' imperfect surfaces of things,
> Threw half an image on the straining eye.
> While wavering woods, and villages, and streams,
> And rocks, and mountain-tops, that long retained
> Th' ascending gleam, were all one swimming scene,
> Uncertain if beheld————————————

We could just discern, through the dimness of the night, the shadowy forms of the mountains, sometimes blotting out half the
sky.

fky, on one fide; and fometimes winding round, as a gloomy barrier on the other.

Often too the road would appear to dive into fome dark abyfs, a cataract roaring at the bottom: while the mountain-torrents on every fide rufhed down the hills in notes of various cadence, as their quantities of water, the declivities of their fall, their diftances, or the intermiffion of the blaft, brought the found fuller, or fainter to the ear; which organ became now more alert, as the imagination depended rather on it, than on the eye, for information.

Thefe various notes of water-mufic, anfwering each other from hill to hill, were a kind of tranflation of that paffage in the pfalms, in which *one deep* is reprefented *calling another becaufe of the noife of the water-pipes.*

Among other images of the night, a lake (for the lake of Baffenthwait was now in view) appeared through the uncertainty of the gloom, like fomething of ambiguous texture, fpreading a lengthened gleam of wan, dead light under the dark fhade of the incumbent mountains: but whether this light

were

were owing to vapours arifing from the valley; or whether it was water—and if water, whether it was an arm of the fea, a lake, or a river—to the uninformed traveller would appear matter of great uncertainty. Whatever it was, it would feem fufficient to alarm his apprehenfions; and to raife in his fancy, (now in queft of dangers,) the idea of fomething, that might ftop his farther progrefs.

A good turnpike-road, on which we entered near the village of Lorton, and a knowledge of the country, fet at nought all fuch ideas with us: but it may eafily be conceived, that a traveller, wandering in the midft of a ftormy night, in a mountainous country, unknown, and unbeaten by human footfteps, might feel palpitations of a very uneafy kind.

We have in Offian fome beautiful images, which accompany a night-ftorm in fuch a country as this. I fhall fubjoin, with a few alterations, an extract from them; as it will illuftrate the fubject before us. It is contained in a note on *Croma*; in which feveral bards are introduced entertaining their patron with their refpective defcriptions of the night.

The

The ſtorm gathers on the tops of the mountains; and ſpreads it's black mantle before
the moon. It comes forward in the majeſty
of darkneſs, moving upon the wings of the
blaſt. It ſweeps along the vale, and nothing
can withſtand it's force. The lightning from
the rifted cloud flaſhes before it: the thunder
rolls among the mountains in it's rear.

All nature is reſtleſs, and uneaſy.

The ſtag lies wakeful on the mountain-
moſs: the hind cloſe by his ſide. She hears
the ſtorm roaring through the branches of the
trees. She ſtarts—and lies down again.

The heath-cock lifts his head at intervals;
and returns it under his wing.

The owl leaves her unfiniſhed dirge; and
ſits ruffled in her feathers in a cleft of the
blaſted oak.

The famiſhed fox ſhrinks from the ſtorm,
and ſeeks the ſhelter of his den.

The hunter alarmed, leaps from his pallet
in the lonely hut. He raiſes his decaying
fire. His wet dogs ſmoke around him. He
half-opens his cabin-door, and looks out:
but he inſtantly retreats from the terrors of
the night.

For

For now the whole ftorm defcends. The mountain torrents join their impetuous ftreams. The growing river fwells.

The benighted traveller paufes as he enters the gloomy dell. The glaring fky difcovers at intervals the terrors of the fcene. With a face of wild defpair he looks round. He recollects neither the rock above, nor the precipice below.—He ftops.—Again he urges his bewildered way. His fteed trembles at the frequent flafh. The thunder burfts over his head—The torrents roar aloud.—He attempts the rapid ford.—Heard you that fcream?—It was the fhriek of death.

How tumultuous is the bofom of the lake! The waves lafh it's rocky fide. The boat is brimful in the cove. The oars are dafhed againft the fhore.

What melancholy fhade is that fitting under the tree on the lonely beach?—I juft difcern it faintly fhadowed out by the pale beam of the moon, paffing through a thin-robed cloud.—It is a female form.—Her eyes are fixed upon the lake. Her hair floats loofe around her arm, which fupports her penfive head.——Ah! mournful maid! doft thou

ftill

ftill expect thy lover over the lake?—Thou
faweft his diftant boat, at the clofe of day,
dancing upon the feathery waves.—Thy breaft
throbs with fufpence: but thou knoweft not
yet, that he lies a corpfe upon the fhore.

S E C T. XVII.

AFTER a wet, and ftormy night we re-
joiced to fee the morning arife with
all the figns of a calm and fplendid day. We
wifhed for the opportunity of furveying Ullefwater in ferene, bright weather. This was
the next fcene we propofed to vifit; and with
which we intended to clofe our views of this
picturefque country.

From Kefwick we mounted a hill, on the
great turnpike road to Penrith. At the fummit we left our horfes; and went to examine
a Druid temple, in a field on the right. The
diameter of this circle is thirty-two *paces*;
which, as nearly as could be judged from
fo inaccurate a mode of menfuration, is the
diameter of Stonehenge; which I once mea-
fured

fured in the fame way. But the ftructures are very different; tho the diameters may be nearly equal. The ftones here are diminutive in comparifon with thofe on Salifbury-Plain. If Stonehenge were a cathedral in it's day; this circle was little more than a country church.

Thefe ftructures, I fuppofe, are by far the moft ancient veftiges of architecture (if we may call them architecture) which we have in England. Their rude workmanfhip hands down the great barbarity of the times of the Druids: and furnifhes ftrong proof of the favage nature of the religion of thefe heathen priefts. Within thefe magical circles we may conceive any incantations to have been performed; and any rites of fuperftition to have been celebrated. It is hiftory, as well as poetry, when Offian mentions the *circles of ftones*, where our anceftors, in their nocturnal orgies, invoked the fpirits which rode upon the winds—the awful forms of their deceafed forefathers; through which, he fublimely tells us, *the ftars dimly twinkled*.

As

As fingular a part as the Druids make in the ancient hiftory, not only of Britain, but of other countries, I know not, that I ever faw any of their tranfactions introduced as the fubject of a capital picture. That they can furnifh a fund of excellent imagery for poetry we know: and I fee not why the fcenes of Caractacus might not be as well fuited to picturefque, as dramatic reprefentation.—And yet there is a difference. The drama depends at leaft as much on fentiment, as on reprefentation. Whereas the picture depends intirely on the latter. The beautiful fentiments of the poet are loft; and the fpectator muft make out the dialogue, as he is able, from the energetic looks of the figures.—Hence therefore it follows, that the fame fubjects are not equally calculated to fhine in poetry, and in painting.

Thofe fubjects, no doubt, are beft adapted to the pencil, which *unfold themfelves by action.* In general, however, all animated ftories, which admit either of *ftrong action,* or *paffion,* are judicioufly chofen. Unanimated fubjects have little chance of producing an effect; particularly

cularly love-ftories; which, of all others, I could wifh to exclude from canvas. The language of love is fo difficult to tranflate, that I know not that I ever faw a *reprefentation* of lovers, who were not ftrongly marked with the character of fimpletons.

But befides fuch fubjects, as admit of ftrong *action,* or *paffion,* there are others of a more *inanimate* caft, which, through the *peculiarity* of the characters, of which they confift, can never be miftaken. Such is the fettlement of Penfylvania, painted by Mr. Weft. From the mixture of Englifh, and Indian characters, and a variety of appofite appendages, the ftory is not only well told; but, as every picturefque ftory fhould be told, it is obvious at fight.

Among fubjects of this kind, are thofe, which occafioned this digreffion—druidical fubjects. I know few of the *lefs animated kind,* which would admit more picturefque embellifhment, than a Druid-facrifice. The peculiar character, and favage features of thefe barbarous priefts—their white, flowing veftments—the branch of mifleto, which they hold—the circular ftones (if they could be brought into compofition)—the fpreading oak
—the

—the altar beneath it—and the milk-white
fteer—might all together form a good picture.

I have often admired an etching by Teipolo,
which I have always conceived to be a reprefentation of this fubject.* He does not indeed introduce all the circumftances of a
Druid-facrifice, which I have here enume-
rated: but the characters are fuch, as exactly
fuit the fubject; and the whole feems to be
an excellent illuftration of it.

After we left the temple of the Druids,
we met with little which engaged our attention.
till we came to the *vale of St. John*. This
fcene appeared from the ftand, where we
viewed it, to be a circular area, of about fix,
or feven miles in circumference. It is furrounded intirely by mountains; and is watered
by a fmall river, called the Grata.

The vale of St. John is efteemed one of the
moft celebrated fcenes of beauty in the coun-

---

* It is contained in a book of etchings on emblematical
fubjects.

try:

try: but it did not anfwer our expectation. The ground, confifting of patches of fenced meadow, adorned with farm-houfes, and clumps of trees, was beautifully tumbled about in many parts: but the whole was rather rich, than picturefque: and on this account, I fuppofe, it hath obtained it's celebrity. It's circular form, every where within the fcope of the eye, wanted that variety, which the *winding* vale affords; where one part is continually receding from another in all the pleafing gradations of perfpective.*

The *kind* of fcenery here, is much the fame, as in the vale of Lorton: both are compofed of rural objects; but thefe objects are differently prefented. In the vale of Lorton, the houfes, and hamlets, feated on a wandering ftream, are confined to the fame level; and appear of courfe, *one after another*, as fo many little *feparate landfcapes.* Here they are fcattered about the inequalities of the ground, through the area of a vale, circular at leaft in appearance; and offer the eye *too much at once*—a *confufion*, rather than a *fuc-*

* See the fame idea applied to water, page 184. Vol. I.

ceffion,

ceſſion, of ſcenery. I ſpeak however only of
the *general appearance* of the vale: it contains
undoubtedly many beautiful ſcenes, if we had
had time to explore them.

The plan, or ground-plot, of the vale of
Tempe, as we have it deſcribed by ancient
authors, was ſomewhat ſimilar to this of St.
John. Nature ſeems in both to have wrought
on the ſame model; excepting only that the
furniture of that very celebrated ſcene of antiquity was probably more picturefque.

The vale of Tempe, like this, was circular,
and incompaſſed with mountains. But it's
area was compoſed of level lawns, (at leaſt,
we ſuppoſe, not riſing uniformly before the
eye,) interſperſed with wood; which in many
parts was thick, and cloſe; and muſt every
where have intercepted ſome portion of the
mountain-line, and broken the regularity of
a circular *ſhape*.

The mountains too in Tempe were of a
more beautiful ſtructure; abrupt, hung with
rock, and finely adorned with wood.—At
the head of the vale was a grand, rocky
chaſm, ſhaded with a profuſion of woody

　　　　ſcenery;

fcenery; through which the whole weight of the river Peneus forced it's way, with a tremendous found: and having been dafhed into foam and vapours by the fall, reunited it's ftrength at the bottom, and poured through the vale in a wild, impetuous torrent, roaring over rocks and fhelves, till it found an exit, through the folding of the mountains on the oppofite fide.

Elian indeed tells us, that the ftream was fmooth: but as Ovid's defcription is more picturefque, the reader will give me leave to confider his authority as more decifive. His view of Tempe is very noble: but as he meant principally to defcribe the palace of a river god, which lay among the caverns, and receffes of the rocky chafm at the entrance of the vale, his fubject naturally led him to dwell chiefly on the cafcade, which was undoubtedly the greateft ornament of the place.

Eft nemus Æmoniæ, prærupta quod undique claudit
Silva: vocant Tempe: per quæ Peneus ab imo
Effufus Pindo, fpumofis volvitur undis;
Dejectuque gravi tenues agitantia fumos
Nubila conducit; fummafque afpergine filvas
Impluit: & fonitu plus quam vicina fatigat.
Hæc domus, hæ fedes, hæc funt penetralia magni
Amnis: in hoc refidens facto de cautibus antro,
Undis jura dabat.————

A vale

A vale thus circumftanced is fo pleafing,
that other poets have feized the idea in their
defcriptions.   I could multiply quotations:
but I fhall felect two, in which the fame
fubject is treated in a different manner.   In
one the natural grandeur of the fcene is foftened by little circumftances of chearfulnefs:
in the other, it ftrikes in the full majefty
of the fublime.   The former is more the
vale of St. John: the latter approaches nearer
the idea of the Theffalian vale.

> Into a foreft far they thence him led,
> Where was their dwelling in a pleafant glade,
> With mountains round about invironed.
> And mighty woods that did the valley fhade,
> And like a ftately theatre it made,
> Spreading itfelf into a fpacious plain.
> And in the midft a little river played
> Amongft the pumy ftones, which feemed to plain,
> With gentle murmur that his courfe they did reftrain.

> —————————————The hills
> Of Æta, yielding to a fruitful vale,
> Within their range half-circling had inclofed
> A fair expanfe in verdure fmooth.   The bounds
> Were edged by wood, o'erhung by hoary cliffs,
> Which from the clouds bent frowning.   Down a rock,
> Above the loftieft fummit of the grove,

A tumbling

A tumbling torrent wore the fhagged ftone;
Then gleaming through the intervals of fhade,
Attained the valley, where the level ftream
Diffufed refrefhment————

The vale of St. John was, fome years ago, the fcene of one of thofe terrible inundations, which wafted lately the vale of Brackenthwait. I fhall relate the circumftances of it, as they were given us on the fpot: but as we had them not perhaps on the beft authority, they may, in fome particulars, be overcharged.

It was on the 22d of Auguft 1749, that this difafter happened. That day, which had been preceded by weather uncommonly clofe and fultry, fet in with a gloomy afpect. The blacknefs gathered, more, and more, from every quarter. The air was hot beyond fufferance. The whole atmofphere glowed, and every thing around was in a ftate of perfect ftagnation. Not a leaf was in motion.

In the mean time, the inhabitants of the vale heard a ftrange noife in various parts around them: but whether it was in the air, or whether it arofe from the mountains, they could not afcertain. It was like the hollow

murmur

murmur of a rifing wind, among the tops of trees. This noife (which in a fmaller degree is not an uncommon prelude to a ftorm) continued without intermiffion about two hours; when a tempeft of wind, and rain, and thunder, and lightning fucceeded; which was violent, beyond any thing, remembered in former times; and lafted, without paufe, near three hours.

During this ftorm the cataract fell upon the mountain, on the north of the vale; or as fome people thought, tho I fhould fuppofe without any probability, burft from the bowels of it. The fide of that mountain is a continued precipice, through the fpace of a mile. This whole tract, we were told, was covered in an inftant, with one continuous cafcade of roaring torrent (an appearance which muft have equalled the fall of Niagara) fweeping all before it from the top of the mountain to the bottom. There, like that other inundation, it followed the channel of the brooks it met with; and fhewed fimilar effects of it's fury.

One of thefe effects was aftonifhing. The fragments of rock, and deluges of ftone, and fand, which were fwept from the mountain

by

by the torrent, choked one of the ftreams, which received it at the bottom. The water, thus pent up, and receiving continually vaft acceffion of ftrength, after rolling fullenly about that part of the vale in frightful whirl-pools, at length forced a new channel through a folid rock, which we were informed, it disjointed in fome fractured crevice, and made a chafm at leaft ten feet wide. Many of the fragments were carried to a great diftance; and fome of them were fo large, that a dozen horfes could not move them. We were forry afterwards, that we had not feen this remarkable chafm : but we had not time to go in queft of it.

From the vale of St. John we afcended a fteep hill, called Branthwait-cragg; where being obliged to leave the great road in our way to Ullefwater, and inveftigate a pathlefs defert over the mountains, which invironed us; we put ourfelves under the conduct of a guide.

Thefe mountains were covered with a pro-fufion of huge ftones, and detached rocks; among which we found many old people,

and

and children, from the neighbouring villages, gathering a fpecies of white lychen, that grows upon the craggs; and which we heard had been found very ufeful in dying a murray-colour.

Among the difficulties of our rout over thefe mountains, the bogs and moraffes we met with, were the moft troublefome. We were often obliged to difmount; and in fome parts the furface could hardly bear a man. Where rufhes grew, our guide informed us, the ground was firmeft. We endeavoured therefore, as much as poffible, to make the little tuffocks of thefe plants the bafis of our footfteps. But as we could not convey this intelligence to our horfes, they often plunged very deep.

In feveral parts of our ride, we had a view of that grand clufter of mountains, which forms a circle in the heart of Cumberland; and makes a back-ground to the views in almoft every part of the extremities of that county. Thefe mountains unite on the fouth with thofe of Weftmoreland. The fide next us was compofed of Skiddaw.—Threlkate-

fell,

fell, a part of which is called Saddle-back—
and Grifedale-fell.   As we rode nearer the
northern limit of this chain, Skiddaw, which
is by much the higheft mountain, appeared
in perfpective, the leaft.   Behind thefe mountains arife, in order, Mofedale-fell—Carric—
and Caudbeck—the tops of which we fometimes faw, from the higher grounds, peering,
in their blue attire, over the concave parts
of the browner mountains, which ftood nearer
the eye.

Between us, and this circular chain, which
occupied the whole horizon on the left, was
fpread a very extenfive vale; ftretching from
fide to fide hardly lefs than feven or eight
miles; and in length winding out of fight.
It affords little beauty, except what arifes
from the gradations of diftance: but it fuggefts an idea of greatnefs; which fpace, and
grand boundaries, however unadorned, will
always fuggeft.

This idea hath fometimes mifled the taftlefs
improver of little fcenes.   He has heard, that
fpace gives beauty; but not knowing how to
accommodate the rule to circumftances, he
often

often fhews all that is to be feen; when, in fact, he fhould have hid half of it, as a deformity. *Mere* fpace gives the idea of *grandeur*, rather than of *beauty*. Such an idea the ocean prefents. But a *little* fcene cannot prefent it. *Grandeur* therefore is not attained by attempting it; while *beauty* is often loft.

. Along this vale ran the great road we had juft left; which was no little ornament to it. The mazy courfe of a river is a ftill nobler object of the fame kind: but a great road is no bad fubftitute; and is in fome refpects fuperior. The *river* being on a level, and contained within banks, is generally too much hid, unlefs it be viewed from an elevated point. But the *road* following the inequalities of the ground, is eafily traced by the eye, as it winds along the feveral elevations, and depreffions it meets with; and has therefore more variety in it's courfe.

On the right, forming the other fide of this extenfive vale, arife feveral very high
moun-

mountains; among which Hara-fide, and White-pike are the moft magnificent. At the bottom of thefe, verging towards the fkirts of the vale, are other hills lefs formidable: but two of them, called the Mell-fells, are very remarkable; being fhaped like earthen graves, in a country church-yard.

A little before we approached the Mell-fells, the path we purfued led us under a towering rocky hill, which is known by the name of *Wolf's-cragg;* and is probably one of the monuments of this animal in Britain. It is a fortrefs intirely adapted to a garrifon of wolves; from whence they might plun-der the vale which was fpread before them: and make prey of every thing, as far as the eye could reach. Such a landfcape, in painting, would be highly characterized by fuch appendages. It would have pleafed Ridinger. If that picturefque naturalift had been in queft of a wolf-fcene, he could not have found a better.

When

When we had paffed this range of mountains, we got more into a beaten path, leading to the village of Matterdale, about a
mile only from Ullefwater; which was ftill
intirely excluded from our fight by high
grounds. Here we difmiffed our guide, and
were directed into Gobray-park, which is
the northern boundary of the lake.

This part of the country we found well
inhabited : and the roads, at this feafon, much
frequented. It was about the time of a fta-
tute-fair; when the young people of the feveral villages leave their old fervices, and go
to their new: and we were not a little entertained with the fimplicity, and variety of
the different groups and figures we met, both
on horfeback, and on foot.

Thefe are the picturefque inhabitants of a
landfcape. The dreffed-out figures, and gaudy
carriages, along the great roads of the capital,
afford them not. The pencil rejects with
indignation the fplendor of art. In grand
fcenes, even the peafant cannot be admitted,

if

if he be employed in the low occupations of his profeffion: the fpade, the fcythe, and the rake are all excluded.

Moral, and picturefque ideas do not alwas coincide. In a moral light, cultivation, in all it's parts, is pleafing; the hedge, and the furrow; the waving corn field, and rows of ripened fheaves. But all thefe, the picturefque eye, in queft of fcenes of grandeur, and beauty, looks at with difguft. It ranges after nature, untamed by art, and burfting wildly into all it's irregular forms.

————————————Juvat arva videre
Non raftris hominum, non ulli obnoxia curæ.

It is thus alfo in the introduction of figures. In a moral view, the induftrious mechanic is a more pleafing object, than the loitering peafant. But in a picturefque light, it is otherwife. The arts of induftry are rejected; and even idlenefs, if I may fo fpeak, adds dignity to a character. Thus the lazy cowherd refting on his pole; or the peafant lolling on a rock, may be allowed in the grandeft fcenes; while the laborious mechanic, with his implements of labour, would be repulfed.

The

The fisherman, it is true, may follow his
calling upon the lake: but he is indebted
for this privilege, not to his art; but to
the picturesque apparatus of it—his boat, and
his nets, which qualify his art. *They* are the
objects: *he* is but an appendage. Place him
on the shore, as a single figure, with his rod,
and line; and his art would ruin him. In a
chearful glade, along a purling brook, near
some mill, or cottage, let him angle, if he
please: in such a scene the picturesque eye
takes no offence. But let him take care not
to introduce the vulgarity of his employment
in a scene of grandeur.

At the same time, we must observe, that
figures, which thus take their importance
merely from not mixing with low, mechanic
arts, are at best only *picturesque appendages.*
They are of a negative nature, neither adding
to the grandeur of the idea, nor taking from
it. They merely and simply *adorn* a scene.

The characters, which are most *suited to
these scenes* of grandeur, are such as impress
us with some idea of greatness, wildness, or
ferocity; all which touch on the sublime.

Figures

Figures in long, folding draperies; gypfies; banditti; and foldiers,—not in modern regimentals; but as Virgil paints them;

————longis adnixi haftis, et fcuta torientos;

are all marked with one or other, of thefe characters: and mixing with the magnificence, wildnefs, or horror of the place, they properly coalefce; and reflecting the fame images, add a deeper tinge to the character of the fcene.

For the truth of all thefe remarks! I might appeal to the decifive judgment of Salvator Rofa; who feems to have thoroughly ftudied propriety in figures, efpecially in fcenes of grandeur. His works are a model on this head. We have a book of figures, particularly compofed for fcenery of this kind, and etched by himfelf. In this collection there is great variety, both in the characters, groups, and dreffes: but I do not remember, either there, or in any other of his works, a low, mechanic character. All his figures are either of (what I have called) the *negative* kind; or marked with fome trait of *greatnefs, wildnefs,* or *ferocity.* Of this laft fpecies his figures

gene-

generally partook : his grand scenes being inhabited chiefly by banditti.

I met with a passage, not a little illustra-
tive of these remarks on figures, in the travels of Mr. Thicknefs through Spain.

" The worst fort of beggars, says he,
in Spain are the troops of male, and female
gypsies. They are of the genuine breed, and
differ widely from all other gypsies ; and I
may fay, from all other human beings. I
often met troops of these people ; and when
an interview happens in roads very distant
from towns, or dwellings, it is not very pleafing : for they ask, as if they knew they were
not to be refused ; and I dare fay often commit murders, when they can commit them
by surprize. They are extremely swarthy,
with hair as black as jet ; and form very picturesque groups under the shade of the rocks
and trees of the Pyrænean mountains, where
they spend their evenings : and live suitably
to the climate ; where bread, and water, and
idlenefs, are preferable to better fare, and
hard-labour."

SECT.

S E C T. XVIII.

ON descending the hill from Matterdale, before we came to the lake, we had a beautiful *specimen* (as the naturalists speak) of what in this country is called a *gill*. The road carried us along the edge of one of it's precipices: but the chasm was so intirely filled with wood, that when we looked down, we could not see into it. Even the sun-beams, unable to enter, rested only on the tufted foliage of the trees, which grew from the sides.—But tho the eye was excluded, the ear was soothed by the harmony of an invisible torrent; whose notes, sounding along innumerable broken falls, and softened by ascending through the trees, were very melodious.

A winding road brought us to the bottom; where the torrent tumbling out of the wood,

E re-

received us. We had a fhort view into the deep receffes of the fcene, through the branches of the trees, which ftretched over the ftream; but we had not time to penetrate it's alluring fhade.

Having paffed over more high grounds, we came at length in view of the lake. The firft catch of it was thus prefented.

A road occupied the neareft part of the landfcape, winding around a broken cliff; which rofe confiderably on the left. A portion of a diftant mountain appeared on the right, with a fmall part of the lake at it's foot. The compofition, as far as it went, was correct: but we yet faw only enough to excite our curiofity; and to gives us, from the bearing of the land, a general idea of the lake.

Ullefwater is the largeft lake in this country, except Windermere; being eight miles long; and about two broad in the wideft part; tho, in general, it rarely exceeds a mile in breadth.

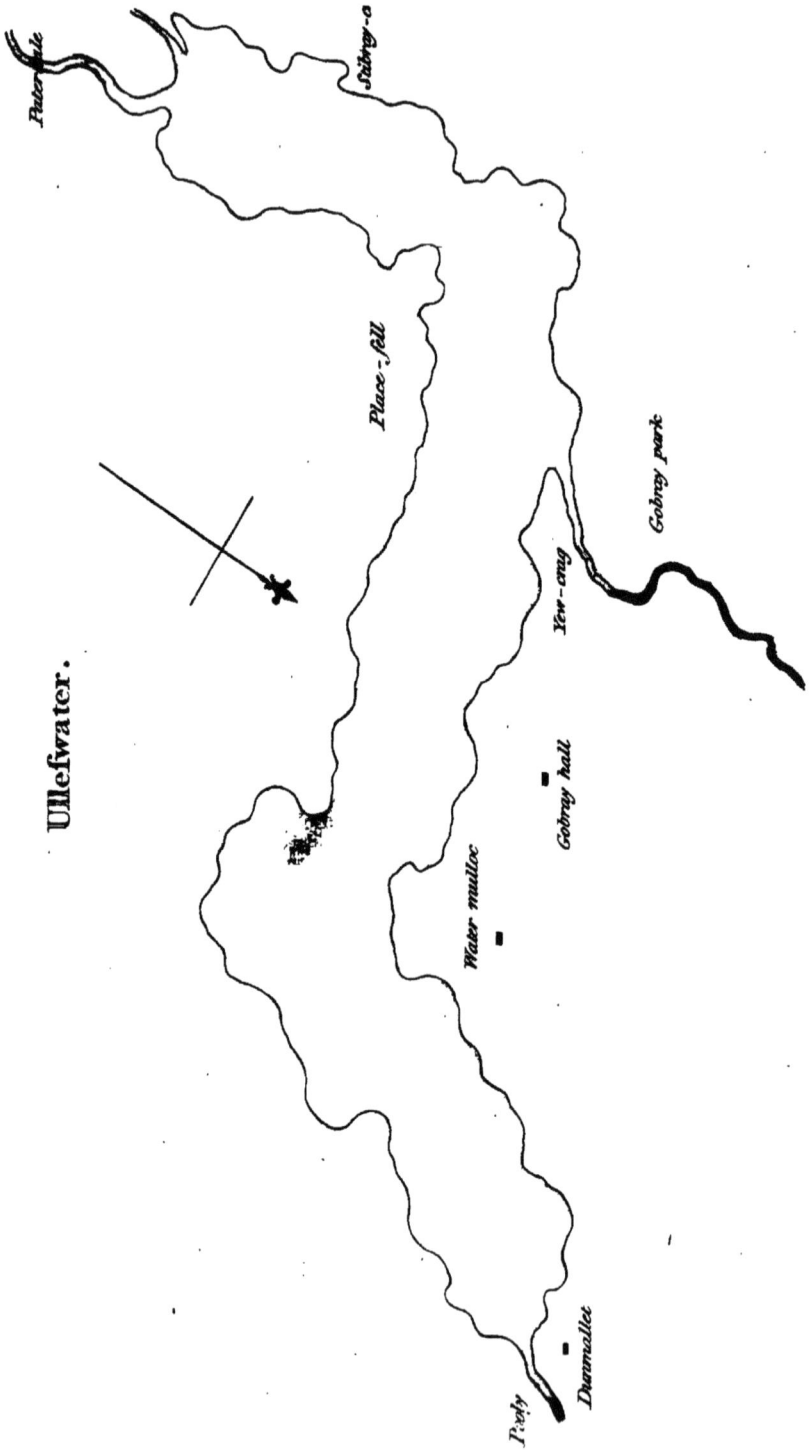

Ullefwater.

Patterdale

Stibray-o

Place-fell

Gobray park

Yew-crag

Gobray hall

Water mulloc

Poely

Darmullet

breadth. It points nearly north, and south; as most of these lakes do; but being placed at an *extremity* of the barrier-mountains, it affords a greater variety than is exhibted by such lakes, as are *invironed* by them. These having few accompaniments, receive their character chiefly from the surrounding desolation. Such a lake is Wyburn. Windermere, on the other hand, Keswick, Butermer, and Ullefwater may all be called *boundary-lakes*. One end of each participates more of the rugged country; and the other of the cultivated: tho each end participates, in some degree, of both. A few traits of romantic scenery are added to the tameness of one end; while the native horror of the other is softened by a few chearful appendages.

The form of Ullefwater resembles a Z; only there is no angular acuteness in it's line. It spreads every where in an easy curve; beautifully broken in some parts by promontories. —The middle reach contains in length near two thirds of the lake. The southern side is mountainous; and becomes more so, as it verges towards the west. As the mountains approach the north, they glide (as we have feen is usual in *boundary-lakes*) into meadows

and

and pastures. The northern and western sides
contain a great variety of woody and rocky
scenes; but these also, as they approach the
east, become smooth and fertilized. At the
southern point, under impending mountains,
lies the village of Patterdale.—With this general idea of Ulleswater, let us return to the
descent from Matterdale, where we caught the
first view of it.

As we descended a little farther, the whole
scene of the lake opened before us; and such a
scene, as almost drew from us the apostrophe
of the inraptured bard,

> Visions of glory, spare my aching sight!

Among all the *visions* of this inchanting
country, we had seen nothing so beautifully
sublime, so correctly picturesque as this.—
And yet I am averse to make comparisons;
especially on seeing a country but once. Much
depends on the circumstances of light, and
weather. I would wish therefore only to say,
that I was *more pleased* with Ulleswater, than
with any lake I had seen; adding, at the same
time, that we were fortunate in a concurrence

of

of incidents, that aided it's beauty. We had
hitherto feen all the lakes we had vifited, under
a rough, or cloudy fky: and tho their dignity
was certainly increafed by that circumftance;
yet the beauty of a lake in fplendid, ferene
weather, aided, at this time, by the powers of
contraft, made a wonderful impreffion on the
imagination. The impreffion might have been
the fame, if Ullefwater had been the firft lake,
we had feen in a ftorm.

" The effect of the *fublime*, fays Mr. Burke,
is *aftonifhment*; and the effect of *beauty*, is *pleafure*: but when the two ingredients mix, the
effect is in a good meafure deftroyed in both.
They conftitute a fpecies fomething different
both from the fublime and beautiful, which I
have before called *fine*: but this kind, I imagine, has not fuch a power on the paffions,
either as vaft bodies have, which are endowed
with the correfpondent qualities of the fublime;
or as the qualities of beauty have, when united
in a fmall object. The affection produced by
large bodies, adorned with the fpoils of beauty,

is

is a tention continually relieved; which approaches to the nature of mediocrity *.

This refined reasoning does not seem intirely
grounded on experience.—I do not remember
any scene in which beauty and sublimity, according to my ideas, are more blended than in
this: and tho Mr. Burke's ideas of beauty
are perhaps more exceptionable, than his ideas
of the sublime; yet it happens, that most of
the qualities, which he predicates of both,
unite in this scene. Their effect therefore, according to his argument, should be destroyed.
But the feelings of every lover of nature, on
viewing these scenes, I dare say, would revolt
from such reasoning. Ours certainly did.

The foreground of the grand view before us,
is a part of Gobray-park, which belongs to the
duke of Norfolk: rough, broken, and woody.
Among the old oaks, which inriched it, herds
of deer, and cattle grazed in groups. Beyond
this is spread an extensive reach of the lake,
winding round a rocky promontory on the left;

---

* Sublime and Beautiful, Part IV. Sect. 25.

which

which is the point of a mountain, called Martindale-fell, or Place-fell: the fouthern boundary of the lake. This promontory uniting
with the mountain, lets it eafily down into
the water, as by a ftep. An *hefitation*, if I
may fo call it, of this kind, eafes greatly the
heavinefs of a line. In a *diftance*, it is of lefs
confequence: but in all the *nearer* grounds,
it is neceffary. I fpeak chiefly however of
thofe views, in which beauty, and grandeur are
combined. In thofe of fimple grandeur, and
fublimity, as in that of Penmanmaur, for inftance, in north Wales, the heavy line, which
is very remarkable in that fcene, from the Irifh
road, perhaps ftrengthens the effect.

Martindale-fell is entirely unplanted; but it's
line, and furface are both well varied. Numberlefs breaks (little vallies, and knolls) give it
a lightnefs, without injuring it's fimplicity.

Such was the difpofition of the objects, on
the left of the lake: on the right, two woody
promontories, purfuing each other in perfpective, made a beautiful contraft with the fmooth
continuity of Martindale-fell.

In front, the diftance was compofed of
mountains, falling gently into the lake; near

the

the edge of which lies the village of Patterdale.

We took this view at a point, which had
juft fo much elevation, as to give a variety to
the lines of the lake. As we defcended to the
water, the view was ftill grand, and beautiful,
but had loft fome of it's more picturefque
beauties: it had loft the foreground: it had
loft the fweeping line round the mountain on
the left; and it had loft the recefs between
the two woody promontories on the right.
The whole margin of the lake was nearly reduced to one ftraight line.—The beauty of a
view, efpecially in lake-fcenery, we have before obferved,* depends greatly on the nice
pofition of it's point.

Having fpent fome time in examining this
very inchanting fcene, we fkirted the lake
towards Patterdale, on a tolerable road, which
runs from one end of it to the other: on the
fouth it is continued to Amblefide; on the
north, to Penrith. I call it a tolerable road;
but I mean only for horfes. It has not the

---

* See page 96. Vol. I,

quartering

quartering and commodious width of a carriage road.

As we left Gobray-park, we took our rout
along the margin of the firft of thofe woody
promontories on the right. We were carried
by the fide of the lake, through clofe lanes,
and thick groves: yet not fo thick, but that
we had every where, through the openings
of the trees, and windings of the road, views
in front, and on the right, into woody receffes; fome of which were very pleafing:
and on the left, the lake, and all it's diftant
furniture, broke frequently upon us.

After fkirting the firft woody promontory,
which carried us about a mile, the road turned
fuddenly to the right, and led us round into
the fecond, rifing a confiderable height above
the water.—In this promontory, a new fcene
opened: the woods became intermixed with
rock; and a great variety of beautiful foregrounds were produced. The rocks, through
which the road was fometimes cut, were
chiefly on our right.—In this promontory alfo,

as well as in the other, we were amused with catches of the lake, and of Martindale-fell, through the trees.

Scenes, like these, are adapted to every state of the sky. They were beautiful in the calm' season, in which we saw them; and in which indeed we wished to see them. But they would have received peculiar advantages also from a storm. The objects are all in that great style, which is suited to the violences of nature. The imagination would have risen with the tempest, and given a double grandeur to every awful form.—The trees, in the mean time, which rear themselves stage above stage, upon the mountain's brow, and spread down to the very road, would have made a noble instrument for the hollow blast to found, consisting of various notes: while the surges of the lake, resounding among the caverns, and dashing against the rocks, many fathoms below, would have aided the concert with new notes of terrific harmony.

————There

——————————————————There is a mood,
(I fing not to the vacant and the young)
There is a kindly mood of melancholy,
That wings the foul, and points her to the fky.
While winds, and tempefts fweep the various lyre,
How fweet the diapafon!————————

The mind is not always indeed in unifon
with fuch fcenes, and circumftances, as thefe.
When it does not happen to be fo, no effect
can be produced. Sometimes indeed the fcene
may draw the mind into unifon; if it be not
under the impreffion of any ftrong paffion of
an oppofite kind; but in a fort of neutral
ftate. The effect however will always be
ftrongeft, when the mind happens to be poffeffed of ideas congenial to the fcene—when,
in a *kindly mood of melancholy*, it feels itfelf
foothed by the objects around.

But befides the mufic of winds and tempefts, the ecchoes, which are excited in different parts of this lake, are ftill more grand,
and affecting. More or lefs they accompany
all lakes, that are circumfcribed by lofty, and
rocky fkreens. We found them on Windermere; we found them on Derwentwater. But
every

every lake, being furrounded by rocks and mountains of a ftructure peculiar to itfelf, forms a variety of inftruments; and, of courfe, a variety of founds. The ecchoes therefore of no two lakes are alike; unlefs they are mere monotonifts.

We took notice of a very grand eccho on the weftern fhores of the great ifland in Windermere: but the moft celebrated ecchoes are faid to be found on Ullefwater; in fome of which the found of a cannon is diftinctly reverberated fix, or feven times. It firft rolls over the head in one vaft peal.—Then fubfiding a few feconds, it rifes again in a grand, interrupted burft, perhaps on the right.— Another folemn paufe enfues. Then the found arifes again on the left.—Thus thrown from rock to rock, in a fort of aerial perfpective, it is caught again perhaps by fome nearer promontory; and returning full on the ear, furprizes you, after you thought all had been over, with as great a peal as at firft.

But the grandeft effect of this kind is produced by a *fucceffive* difcharge of cannon;[*]

---

[*] The duke of Portland, who has property in this neighbourhood, has a veffel on the lake, with brafs guns, for the purpofe of exciting ecchoes.

at

at the interval of a few feconds between each
difcharge. The effect of the firft is not over,
when the ecchoes of the fecond, the third,
or perhaps of the fourth, begin. Such a variety of awful founds, mixing, and commix-
ing, and at the fame moment heard from all
fides, have a wonderful effect on the mind;
as if the very foundations of every rock on the
lake were giving way; and the whole fcene,
from fome ftrange convulfion, were falling,
into general ruin.

: Thefe founds, which are all of the terrific
kind, are fuited chiefly to fcenes of grandeur
during fome moment of wildnefs, when the
lake is under the agitation of a ftorm. In a
calm, ftill evening, the gradations of an eccho,
dying away in diftant thunder, are certainly
heard with moft advantage. But that is a
different idea. You attend then only to the
ecchoes themfelves. When you take the *fcene*
into the combination; and attend to the effect
of the *whole together;* no doubt fuch founds,
as are of the moft violent kind, are beft fuited
to moments of the greateft uproar.

· But there is another fpecies of ecchoes,
which are as well adapted to the lake in all
it's ftillnefs, and tranquillity, as the others

are

are to it's wildness, and confusion: and which recommend themselves chiefly to those feelings, which depend on the gentler movements of the mind. Instead of cannon, let a few French-horns, and clarionets be introduced. Softer music than such loud wind-instruments, would scarce have power to vibrate. The effect is now wonderfully changed. The found of a cannon is heard in bursts. It is the music of thunder. But the *continuation* of *musical founds* forms a *continuation* of *musical ecchoes*; which reverberating around the lake, are exquisitely melodious in their several gradations; and form a thousand symphonies, playing together from every part. The variety of notes is inconceivable. The ear is not equal to their innumerable combinations. It listens to a symphony dying away at a distance; when other melodious founds arise close at hand. These have scarce attracted the attention; when a different mode of harmony arises from another quarter. In short, every rock is vocal, and the whole lake is transformed into a kind of magical scene; in which every promontory seems peopled by aerial beings, answering each other in celestial music.

————How

—————————How often from the fteep
Of ecchoing hill, or thicket, have we heard
Celeftial voices to the midnight air,
Sole, or refponfive each to other's note,
Singing their great Creator? Oft in bands
While they keep watch, or nightly rounding walk,
With heavenly touch of inftrumental founds,
In full harmonic number joined, their fongs
Divide the night, and lift our thoughts to heaven.

Having now almoft fkirted the two woody
promontories in our rout to Patterdale, we
found the conclufion, the grandeft part of the
whole fcenery. It is a bold projection of rock
finely marked, and adorned with hanging
woods; under the beetling fummit of which
the road makes a fudden turn. This is the
point of the fecond promontory; and, I believe, is known by the name of *Stibra-cragg*.
The trees which compofe the whole
fcenery through both thefe promontories, are
in general, oak.

From hence through lanes of the fame
kind, though lefs fuperbly decorated, we
came to the village of Patterdale; fituated
on rifing grounds, among two or three little
rivers,

rivers, or branches of a river, which feed the lake. It lies in a cove of mountains, open in front to the fouthern reach of the lake; beyond which appear the high, woody lands of Gobray-park. The fituation is magnificent.

Among the cottages of this village, ftands a houfe, belonging to a perfon of fomewhat better condition; whofe little eftate, which he occupies himfelf, lies in the neighbourhood. As his property, inconfiderable as it is, is better than that of any of his neighbours, it has gained him the title of *King of Patterdale*, in which his family name is loft. His anceſtors have long enjoyed the title before him. We had the honour of feeing this prince, as he took the diverfion of fifhing on the lake; and I could not help thinking, that if I were inclined to envy the fituation of any potentate in Europe, it would be that of the king of Patterdale. The pride of Windfor and Verſailles would fhrink in a comparifon with the magnificence of his dominions.

The

The great simplicity of this country, and that rigid temperance, and economy, to which neceffity obliges all its inhabitants, may be exemplified by the following little hiftory.

A clergyman, of the name of Mattifon, was minifter of this place fixty years; and died lately at the age of ninety. During the early part of his life, his benefice brought him in only twelve pounds a year. It was afterwards increafed, (I fuppofe by the queen's bounty,) to eighteen; which it never exceeded. On this income he married—brought up four children—lived comfortably among his neighbours—educated a fon, I believe, at the univerfity—and left upwards of one thoufand pounds to his family.—With that fingular fimplicity, and inattention to forms, which characterize a country like this; he himfelf read the burial-fervice over his mother; he married his father to a fecond wife; and afterwards buried him. He publifhed his own banns of marriage in the church, with a woman, whom he had formerly chriftened; and himfelf married all his four children.

From this fpecimen, the manners of the country may eafily be conceived. At a diftance from the refinements of the age, they are at a diftance alfo from its vices. Many fage writers, and Montefquieu * in particular, have fuppofed thefe rough fcenes of nature to have a great effect on the human mind: and have found virtues in mountainous countries, which were not the growth of tamer regions. Many opinions perhaps have paffed current among mankind, with lefs foundation in truth. Montefquieu is in queft chiefly of political virtue—liberty—bravery—and the arts of bold defence: but, I believe, private virtue is equally befriended by thefe rough fcenes. It is the happinefs of thefe people, that they have no great roads among them: and that their fimple villages, on the fides of lakes, and mountains, are in no line of communication with any of the bufy haunts of men. Ignorance is fometimes called the mother of vice. I apprehend it to be as often the nurfe of innocence.

---

* Book XVIII. Ch. II.

Much

Much have thofe travellers to anfwer for, whofe cafual intercourfe with this innocent, and fimple people tends to corrupt them; diffeminating among them ideas of extravagance, and diffipation—giving them a tafte for pleafures, and gratifications, of which they had no ideas—infpiring them with difcontent at home—and tainting their rough, induftrious manners with idlenefs, and a thirft after difhoneft means.

If travellers would frequent this country with a view to examine it's grandeur, and beauty—or to explore it's varied, and curious regions with the eye of philofophy——or, if that could be hoped, to adore the great Creator in thefe his fublimer works—if, in their paffage through it, they could be content with fuch fare as the country produces; or at leaft reconcile themfelves to it by manly exercife, and fatigue (for there is a time, when the ftomach, and the plaineft food will be found in perfect harmony)—if they could thus, inftead of corrupting the manners of an innocent people, learn to amend their own, by feeing in how narrow a compafs the wants of human life may be compreffed—a journey through thefe wild fcenes might be attended perhaps with more improvement, than a journey to Rome, or Paris. Where manners are polifhed into vicious refinement, fimplifying is the beft mode of improving; and the example of innocence is a more inftructive leffon, than any that can be taught by artifts, and literati.

But thefe parts are too often the refort of gay company, who are under no impreffions of this kind—who have no ideas, but of extending the fphere of their amufements—or, of varying a life of diffipation. The grandeur of the country is not taken into the queftion: or, at leaft it is no otherwife confidered, than as affording fome new mode of pleafurable enjoyment. Thus even the diverfions of Newmarket are introduced—diverfions, one would imagine, more foreign to the nature of this country, than any other. A number of horfes are carried into the middle of a lake in a flat boat. A plug is drawn from the bottom: the boat finks, and the horfes are left floating on the furface. In different

ferent directions they make to land; and the
horfe, which arrives fooneft, fecures the prize.

Strenua nos exercet inertia: navibus atque
Quadrigis petimus bene vivere. Quod petis, hic eft:
Eft Ulubris; animus fi te non deficit æquus.

SECT.

S E C T. XIX.

HAVING ſpent two hours at Patterdale, in refreſhing our horſes, and in ſurveying the beauty of it's ſituation; we left it with regret, and ſet out for Penrith.

We had now the whole length of the lake to ſkirt; part of which we had already traverſed in our rout from Gobray-park: but we felt no reluctance at taking a ſecond view of it.

As we traverſed the two woody promontories, which we had paſſed in the morning, we had a grand exhibition of the middle reach of the lake; which, I have obſerved, is by far the longeſt. Martindale-fell, ſhooting into the water, which before adorned the left

of

of the landfcape, now took it's ftation on the right. The left was compofed of the high woody grounds about Gobray-park,—In the center, the hills gently declining, formed a boundary at the bottom of the lake ; ftretching far to the eaft.—As a foreground, we had the woods, and rocks of the two promontories, through which we paffed.

Such were the outlines, and compofition of the view before us ; but it's colouring was ftill more exquifite.

The fun was now defcending low, and caft the broad fhades of evening athwart the land-fcape, while his beams, gleaming with yellow luftre through the vallies, fpread over the in-lightened fummits of the mountains, a thou-fand lovely tints—in fober harmony, where fome deep recefs was faintly fhadowed—in fplendid hue, where jutting knolls, or pro-montories received the fuller radiance of the diverging ray. The air was ftill : the lake, one vaft expanfe of cryftal mirror. The mountain-fhadows, which fometimes give the water a deep, black hue (in many circum-ftances, extremely picturefque ;) were foftened

here

here into a mild, blue tint, which fwept over half the furface. The other half received the fair impreffion of every radiant form, that glowed around. The inverted landfcape was touched in fainter colours, than the real one. Yet it was more than *laid in*. It was al-moft finifhed. The laft touches alone were wanting.

What an admirable ftudy for the pallet is fuch a fcene as this! infinitely beyond the camera's contracted bounds. Here you fee nature in her full dimenfions. You are let into the very myftery—into every artifice, of her pencil. In the *reflected picture*, you fee the *ground fhe lays in*—the great effects pre-ferved—and that veil of expreffive obfcurity thrown over all, in which what is done, is done fo exquifitely, that if you wifh the *finifh-ing touches*, you wifh them only by the fame inimitable hand that gave the fketch. Turn from the fhadow to the reality, and you have them. There the obfcurity is detailed. The picture, and the fketch reflect mutual graces on each other.

I dwell the longer on this view of Ullef-water, becaufe during five days, which we fpent in this romantic country, where we took a

view

view of fo many lakes, this was the only moment, in which we were fo fortunate, as to
fee the water in a *pure*, reflecting ftate. Partial
exhibitions of the kind we had often met
with : but here we were prefented with an
exhibition of this kind in it's utmoft magnificence.

Having examined this very lovely landfcape,
fo perfect both in compofition, and in colouring,
we proceeded in our rout along the lake.

We now re-entered Gobray park; which
afforded us, for near three miles, a great variety of beautiful fcenes on the left, compofed
of rocky, and broken-ground, foreft-trees,
coppfe-wood, and wooded hills : while the
lake, and mountains, whofe fummits were
now glowing with the full fplendor of an
evening fun, were a continued fund of varied
entertainment on the right. The eye was both
amufed, and relieved by furveying the two
different modes of fcenery in fucceffion: the
broad fhades, and bright diverfified tints, of
the diftant mountains, on one fide; and the
beautiful forms, and objects of the foreground,
on the other.

One

One part of the foreground was marked with singular wildness. It was a kind of rocky pass near the margin of the lake; known, I believe, by the name of *Yew-cragg*. If Cæsar had seen it, it would have struck him in a military light; and he would have described it as a defile, "angustum, & difficile, inter montem, & lacum; quo vix singuli carri ducerentur. Mons altissimus impendebat; ut facile perpauci transitum prohibere possent."*

But our imaginations were more amused with picturesque, than military ideas. It struck us therefore merely as an object of beauty.—It's features were these.

At a little distance from the lake, the broken side of a mountain falls abruptly to the ground in two noble tiers of rock; both which are shattered in every direction. The rocks were ornamented in the richest manner with wood. The road skirted the lake; and between it and the rocks, all was rough, broken-ground, intangled with brakes, and impaffable. Among the rocks arose a grove of forest-trees,

---

* Cæf. Com. lib. 1.

of

of various height, according to the inequality of the ground. Here and there, a few scattered oaks, the fathers of the foreft, reared their peeled, and withered trunks across the glade; and fet off the vivid green of the more luxuriant trees. The deer ftarting from the brakes, as the feet of our horfes approached, added new wildnefs to the native character of the view; while the fcreams of a hernery (the wildeft notes in nature) allowed the ear to participate in the effect.

The illumination of this grand mafs of rock was as interefting, as the compofition of it. It was overfpread, when we faw it, with a deep evening-fhadow, with many a darker tint in the clofer receffes. A mild ray, juft tinged with the blufh of a fetting fun, tipped the fummits of the trees:

> While, rufhing through the branches, rifted cliffs
> Dart their *white* heads, and *glitter* through the *gloom.*

Were a man difpofed to turn hermit, I know not where he could fix his abode more agreeably than here. The projecting rocks would
afford

afford a fheltered fituation for his cell; which would open to a fcene every way fitted for meditation. He might wander along the bottom of a mountain; and by the fide of a lake, unfrequented, except by the foot of curiofity; or of fome hafty fhepherd, feeking for the ftragglers of his flock. Here he might enjoy the contemplation of nature in all her fimplicity and grandeur. This fingle land-fcape, the mere invirons of his cell, under all the varieties of light, and fhade—fun-fhine, and ftorm—morning, and evening, would itfelf afford an inexhaufted fund of entertainment: while the ample tome expanded daily before his eye, would banifh the littlenefs of life; and naturally imprefs his mind with great ideas.

From this wild fcene we foon entered another of a different caft. It was a circular plain, about half a mile in diameter; furrounded by mountains, with an opening to the lake. The plain was fmooth, but varied: the mountains, rather low, but rugged.

A valley,

A valley, like this, confidered as a *whole*, has little picturefque beauty. But a picturefque eye will find it's objects even here. It will inveftigate the hills, and pick out fuch portions, as are moft pleafing. Thefe it will form into backgrounds, and inrich the foreground (which can only be a plain) with cattle, trees, or other objects.——Even fuch fimple fcenes, by the aid of judicious lights, may form pictures.

We had the fame kind of view foon after, repeated——a circular valley, furrounded with mountains, tho varied in many particulars from the other. Both however were equally unadorned; and as both were capable, by a few well-chofen accompaniments, of being formed into good pictures; fo likewife both were capable of being made delightful fcenes in nature, by a little judicious planting; tho we muft ftill have wifhed this planting to have had the growth of a century.

It

It is remarkable, that we find fcarce any difpofition of ground, that belongs to a mountainous country, of which Virgil has not taken notice. The fcenes we now examined, he exactly defcribes: only he has given his hills the ornament of wood, which he knew was their moft picturefque drefs.

—————————————————————Tendit
Gramineum in campum, quem collibus undique curvis
Cingebant fylvæ, mediaque in valle theatri
Circus erat.————————————————

Not far from thefe circular plains ftands *Gobray-hall*; once the capital of thefe domains; but now a neglected manfion. If fituation can recommend a place, this feems to enjoy one in great perfection. It ftands on high ground, with higher ftill behind it. We did not ride up to the houfe; but it feemed to command a noble view of the lake, and of the fcenery around it.

Nearly at the point where Ullefwater makes it's laft curve, ftands the village of *Water-Mullock*;

Mullock; fituated rather within the land. Through this place the road carried us to the laft reach of the lake; which is the leaft beautiful part. Here the hills grow fmooth, and lumpifh; and the country, at every ftep, lofes fome of the wild ftrokes of nature; and degenerates, if I may fo fpeak, into cultivation.

At the end of the lake ftands *Dunmallet*, a remarkable hill, which overlooks the laft reach; but is itfelf rather a difgufting object. Shaped with conic exactnefs; planted uniformly with Scotch firs; and cut as uniformly into walks verging to a center, it becomes a vile termination of a noble view.——Once probably it was more interefting; when the Roman eagle was planted, as it formerly was, upon it's fummit—when it's bold, rough fides were in unifon with the objects around—and a noble caftle frowned, from it's precipices over the lake. This fortrefs, whofe ramparts may yet be traced, muft once have been of confiderable importance, as it commanded all the avenues of the country.

We

We had now finiſhed our view of Ullefwater, which contains a wonderful variety
of grand, and picturefque ſcenes, compreſſed
within a very narrow compafs.—In one part,
not far from Water-Mullock, the road carried
us to the higher grounds, from whence
we had a view of the whole lake, and all it's
vaſt accompaniments together—a troubled ſea
of mountains; a broken ſcene—amuſing, but
not picturefque.

In our evening-ride, we had ſkirted only
one ſide of the lake; and wiſhed our time
would have allowed us to ſkirt the other alſo.
It is probable the ſouthern coaſt might have
afforded very noble diſtant views of the woods,
and rocks of Gobray-park, and the adjacent
lofty grounds.

We could have wiſhed alſo to have navi-
gated the lake: for though views from the
water, are in general lefs beautiful, than the
ſame views from the *land*, as they want the

advantage of a foreground, and alſo bring the horizon too low;* yet it is probable the grand reaches of this lake, and the woody promontories, round which the water winds, would have diſplayed many beautiful paſſages from a boat.

One view from the water, we heard much commended, that of the laſt reach of the lake, towards the conic hill of Dunmallet. The ſides of the lake—it's gliding away into the river Eamot, which carries it off—Pooly-bridge, which is thrown over that river, at the bottom of the lake—and the country beyond—were all much extolled: but we could not conceive, that any views, at this end of the lake, could be comparable to what we had ſeen near the ſhores of Patterdale: eſpecially any views, in which the regular form of Dunmallet made ſo conſiderable a part.

It would have added alſo to our amuſement, to have taken a view of the lake by moon-

---

* See page 96. Vol. I.

light.

light. For tho it is very difficult *in painting* to manage fo feeble an effufion of light in fuch a manner, as, at the fame time, to *illumine objects*, and *produce an effect*; yet the *reality*, in fuch fcenes as these, is attended often with a wonderful folemnity and grandeur. That fhadowy form of great objects, which is fometimes traced out by a filver thread, and fometimes by a kind of bright obfcurity on a darker ground, almoft oppreffes the imagination with fublime ideas. Effects alfo we fometimes fee of light and fhade, tho only faintly marked. In the abfence of colour, the clair-obfcure is more ftriking:

————————one expanded fheet of light
Diffufing: while the fhades (from rock to rock
Irregularly thrown, with folemn gloom
Diverfify the whole.————————

I cannot leave the fcenes of Ullefwater, without taking notice of an uncommon fifh, which frequents it's waters; and which is equally the object of the naturalift, and of the epicure. It is of the trout-fpecies; beauti-tifully clad in fcales of filver; firm, and finely

flavoured;

flavoured; and of such dimensions, that it has sometimes been known to weigh between thirty, and forty pounds.

Having now past the limits of the lake, we traversed a very pleasant country in our road to Penrith, keeping the Eamot commonly within view on our right; and leaving on the left, the ruins of Dacre-castle, the ancient seat of the noble family of that name.

No part of Cumberland is more inhabited by the genteeler families of the county than this. Within the circumference of a few miles stand many of their houses; some of which have formerly been castles: but the road carried us in view only of two or three of them.

Before we arrived at Penrith, one of these fortresses, which is known by the name of Penrith-castle, presented us with a very noble ruin; and under the most interesting circumstances. The sun, which, through the length

of

of a fummer-day, had befriended us with all his morning, noon, and evening powers; preparing now, with *farewell fweet*, to take his leave, gave us yet one more beautiful exhibition.

A grand broken arch prefented itfelf firft in deep fhadow. Through the aperture appeared a part of the internal ftructure, thrown into perfpective to great advantage; and illumined by the departing ray. Other fragments of the fhattered towers, and battlements were juft touched with the fplendid tint: but the body of light refted on thofe parts, which were feen through the fhadowed arch.

In the offskip, beyond the caftle, arofe a hill, in fhadow likewife; on the top of which ftood a lonely beacon. The windows anfwering each other, we could juft difcern the glowing horizon through them—a circumftance, which however trivial in defcription, has a beautiful effect in landfcape.—This beacon is a monument of thofe tumultuous times, which preceded the union; and the only monument of the kind now remaining in thefe parts; though fuch beacons were formerly ftationed over the whole country;

and

and could fpread intelligence, in a few feconds, from one end of it to the other.

At this later day thefe caftles and pofts of alarm, adorning the country, they once defended, raife pleafing reflections on a comparifon of prefent times with paft—thofe turbulent times, when no man could fleep in fafety unlefs fecured by a fortrefs. In war he feared the invafion of an open enemy: and in peace a mifchief ftill more formidable, the ravages of banditti; with whom the country was always at that time infefted. Thefe wretches were compofed of the outlaws from both nations; and inhabiting the faftneffes of bogs, and mountains, ufed to fally out, and plunder in all directions.

Penrith is a neat town, fituated not unpleafantly, under mountains; and in the neighbourhood of lakes.

In the church-yard we faw an ancient monument, which has occafioned much fpeculation among antiquarians. It confifts of two rough pillars, with four femicircular ftones, fixed in the ground between them. Dr. Todd, an antiquarian of the laft age, found out four wild-

wild-boars, and other ingenious devices, on
the different parts of this monument. We
examined it with attention: but could not
find even the moft diftant refemblance of any
form in nature. The whole furface feemed
to be nothing more than a piece of rough
chiffel-work.——In the church, which is a
handfome, plain ftructure, is placed a ftone,
recording the ravages of the plague among
the feveral towns of this neighbourhood, in
the year 1598.

As we leave Penrith, which is within twenty
miles of Carlifle, we enter that vaft wafte,
called *Inglewood-foreft*, through which we
rode at leaft nine miles; in all which fpace
there is fcarce a tree to be feen; and yet
were it well planted, as it once probably was,
many parts of it might be admired: for the
ground makes bold and noble fwells; the
back fcenery is compofed of a grand fweep
of mountains; and on the left, are diftant
views into a cultivated country.

The mountains, which adorn thefe fcenes,
are the fame we faw, as we left Kefwick;
only the more northern part of that circular
chain

chain is now turned towards us. In this view, the ridge of Saddle-back affumes that fhape, from which it derives it's appellation.

That part of Inglewood-foreft, which lies neareft the town, is known by the name of Penrith-fell, confifting of rough, and hilly grounds. One of the higheft hills is occu-pied by the beacon, of which we had a dif-tant view, as we examined the ruins of Pen-rith-caftle.

On this fpot, in the year 1715, the Cum-berland militia affembled to oppofe the rebels in their march to the fouth. But a militia without difcipline, is never formidable. The whole body fled, as the van of the rebels appeared marching round an oppofite hill.

Nicolfon, bifhop of Carlifle, a ftrenuous man, who had been very inftrumental in bringing them together, and now attended their march; was fo chagrined, and mortified at their behaviour, that in a fit of obftinate vexation, he would not quit the field. The enemy was coming on apace. His fervants rode up to the coach for orders. The bifhop fat mute with indignation. All thoughts of
himfelf

himfelf were loft in the public difgrace. His coachman however, whofe feelings were lefs delicate, thinking the management of affairs, in this interruption of government, now devolved upon him, lafhed his horfes, and carried his mafter off the field.

On the verge of the foreft, at a place called Plumpton, a large Roman ftation (or ftative camp) runs a quarter of a mile, on the right. You trace the ground broken varioufly, where tents, kitchens, and earthen tables probably ftood, not unlike the veftiges of a modern encampment. On the left appear the lines of a fort of confiderable dimenfions, about one hundred and fifty yards fquare, which was once the citadel of this military colony. The ramparts, and ditches may eafily be traced on every fide.

The great road indeed, which we travelled, is intirely Roman; and is laid almoft by a line over the foreft. You feldom fee a *winding* road of Roman conftruction. Their furveyors, and pioneers had no idea of the line of beauty; nor ftood in reverence of any inclofures; but always took the fhorteft cut; making the

Appian

Appian way the model of all their provincial roads.

At Ragmire, about a mile farther, where the road croffes a bog, large wooden frameworks, yet uninjured by time, were lately dug up; which the Romans had laid, as a foundation for their caufey, over that unftable furface.

On leaving Inglewood-foreft, the road enters an enclofed country, in which is little variety, and fcarce an interefting object, till we arrive at Carlifle.

The approach to that city, from the rifing ground, near the little village of Hereby, is grand. The town, which terminates a vifta of a mile in length, takes a very compact form; in which no part is feen, but what makes a handfome appearance. The fquare, and maffy tower of the caftle rifes on the right: in the middle, the cathedral rifes ftill higher; and contiguous to it, on the left, appear the round towers of the citadel; which was built by Henry VIII. in the form of all

his

his caftles on the Hampfhire, and Kentifh coafts.

The beauty however of this approach is foon loft. As we defcend the hill from Hereby, the town finks into the infignificance of it's invirons.

The entrance is ftill beautiful; the road winding to the gate round the towers of the citadel.

S E C T. XX.

FEW towns offer a fairer field to an anti-
quary, than Carlifle. It's origin, and
hiftory, are remote, curious and obfcure. It
was unqueftionably a place of confequence in
Roman times. Severus's wall juft includes
it in the Britifh pale. The veftiges of that
barrier run within half a mile of it's gates;
and it probably figured firft under the character of a fortrefs, on that celebrated rampart.

In after ages it had it's fhare fucceffively
in the hiftory of Saxons, Danes, and Scots;
and during the revolutions of thefe feveral
nations, was the fcene of every viciffitude of
war. It hath been frequently befieged, pillaged, burnt, and rebuilt. Once it lay buried
in it's ruins for the fpace of two centuries.
Rufus brought it again into exiftence. The
prefent town is founded on the veftiges of
former

former towns; which in many parts have raifed the ground within, nearly to the height of the walls. The foundations of a houfe are rarely dug without difturbing the ruins of fome other houfe. It has been the refidence; and it has been the prifon of kings. An old afh-tree is ftill fhewn, near the gate of the caftle; which is faid to have been planted by the unfortunate Mary of Scotland, who fpent a part of her captivity in this fortrefs; whither fhe was foon brought, after her landing at Workington. Many princes alfo have fhed their royal favours on this ancient town; and made it's fortifications their care.

Now all it's military honours are difgraced. Northern commotions are no longer dreaded. It's gates ftand always open; and it's walls, the object of no farther attention, are falling faft into ruin. The firing of a morning and an evening gun from the caftle, which was the laft garrifon-form that remained, hath been difcontinued thefe fix years, to the great regret of the country around, whofe hours of labour it regulated.

But

But I mean not to enter into the hiftory of Carlifle: it concerns me only as an object of beauty. Within it's walls indeed it contains little that deferves notice. The caftle is heavy in all it's parts, as thefe fabrics commonly are. It is too perfect to afford much pleafure to the picturefque eye; except as a remote object, foftened by diftance. Hereafter, when it's fhattered towers, and buttreffes, give a light-nefs to it's parts, it may adorn fome future landfcape.

The cathedral deferves ftill lefs attention. It is a heavy, Saxon pile; and there is nothing about it, that is beautiful; except the eaft-window, which is a rich, and very elegant piece of Gothic ramification.

The *fratry*, as it is called, or chapter-houfe, in the abbey, is the only building that de-ferves notice. On one fide, where it has formerly been connected with the cloyfters, it has little beauty: but on the other, next the deanery, it's proportions and ornaments are elegant. It feems to be of that ftyle of archi-tecture, which prevailed rather before the two later Henries.

But

But though Carlifle furnifhes little amufement within it's walls; yet it adds great
beauty, as a diftant object, to the country
around. Few towns enjoy a better fituation.
It ftands on a rifing ground, in the midft of
meadows, watered by two confiderable rivers;
which flowing on different fides of the city,
unite a little below it; and form the whole
ground-plot, on which it ftands, into a kind
of peninfula. Beyond the meadows, the
ground rifes, in almoft all parts, at different
diftances.

The meadows around it, efpecially along
the banks of the river Eden, want only a
little more wood to make them very beautiful.
In high floods, which happen two or three
times in the courfe of a winter, they exhibit
a very grand fcene. The town appears ftand-
ing out, like a promontory in the midft of a
vaft lake.

The fhort fiege which Carlifle fuftained in the
rebellion of the-year 1745, together with fome
awkward circumftances that attended it, threw
a general

a general odium upon the town; and many believed, among whom was the late duke of Cumberland, that it was very ill-affected to the government. No suspicion was ever more unjust. I dare take upon me to say, there were scarce half a dozen people in the whole place, who wished well to the rebellion.

The following anecdote, known but to few; and totally unknown till many years after the event, will throw some light on it's hasty surrender; which brought disgrace on it's political principles.

When the rebels came before it, it was garrisoned only by two companies of invalids; and two raw, undisciplined regiments of militia. General Wade lay at Newcastle with a considerable force: and the governor of Carlisle informing him, how unprovided he was, begged a reinforcement. The single hope of this relief, enabled the gentlemen of the country, who commanded the militia, to keep their men under arms.

In the mean time the rebels were known to be as ill-prepared for an attack, as the town was for a defence. They had now lain a week before it; and found it was impracticable, for

want

want of artillery, to make any attempt. They feared alfo an interruption from general Wade : and befides, were unwilling to delay any longer their march towards London. Under thefe difficulties, they had come to a refolution to abandon their defign.

At this critical juncture the governor of Carlifle received a letter from general Wade, informing him, he was fo circumftanced, that he could not poffibly fend the reinforcement that had been defired. This mortifying intelligence, tho not publickly known, was however communicated to the principal officers ; and to fome others : among whom was a bufy attorney, whofe name was H——s.

H——s was then addreffing a young lady, the daughter of Mr. F——r, a gentleman of the country ; and to affift his caufe, and give himfelf confequence with his intended father in law, he whifpered to him, among his other political fecrets, the difappointment from general Wade.

The whifper did not reft here. F——r frequented a club in the neighbourhood ; where obferving (in the jollity of a chearful evening) that only friends were prefent, he gave his company the information he had juft received from H——s.

There

There was in that company, one S——d, a
gentleman of fome fortune near Carlifle, who,
tho a known papift, was however at that
time, thought to be of very intire affection to
the government. This man, poffeffed of fuch
a feeret, and wifhing for an opportunity to
ferve a caufe, which he favoured in his heart,
took horfe that very night, after he left the
club-room, and rode directly to the rebel-
camp; which he found under orders to break
up the next morning. He was carried immediately to the duke of Perth, and others of the
rebel leaders, to whom he communicated his
intelligence; and affured them, they might
expect a mutiny in the town, if they continued before it, one day longer. Counter
orders were immediately iffued; and the next
day the Cumberland and Weftmoreland militia
began to mutiny and difperfe: and the town
defended now only by two companies of invalids, was thought no longer tenable. The
governor was tried by a court-martial; and
acquitted: and nobody fuppofed that either
the militia-officers, or their men, were impreffed by any motive worfe than fear.

In

In so variegated a country, as England, there are few parts, which do not afford many pleasing, and picturesque views. The most probable way of finding them, as I observed a little above, is to follow the course of the rivers. About their banks we shall usually find the richest scenery, which the country can produce. This rule we followed in the few excursions, which we had time to make from Carlisle : and first we took a view of the river Cauda.

Near the town this river is broken into so many streams; and throws up, every where, so many barren beds of pebbles, that there is no great beauty in this part of it's course. But above, where higher banks confine it's impetuosity, it becomes more interesting. The vales of Sebergham and Dalston, we heard much commended. The former we did not visit: the latter we followed, many miles, along it's winding course; and found ourselves often in the midst of beautiful scenes; the river being shut up sometimes by close and lofty banks,
and

and fometimes flowing through meadows edged
with wood.

Among other fituations on the Cauda we
were much pleafed with that of Rofe-caftle,
the feat of the bifhop of Carlifle : which ftands
on a gentle rife, in a wide part of the vale;
the river winding round it, in a femi-circular
form, at about half a mile's diftance. The
ground between the caftle, and the river, confifts of beautiful meadows ; and beyond the
river, a lofty bank, winding with it, and well
planted, forms a fweep of hanging wood.
The caftle compofed of fquare towers, tho no
object on the fpot, is a good ornament to the
fcene.

Between Rofe-caftle and Wigton the country abounds with the relicks of Roman in-
campments. At a place, called Chalk-cliff
(which, by the way, is a cliff of red ftone)
this legionary infcription is engraven in the
native rock.

LEG $\overline{\overline{\text{II}}}$ AVG
MILITES FEC.
COH $\overline{\text{III}}$ COH $\overline{\text{IIII}}$

H 3   From

From the Cauda, our next excurfion was along the Eden. On the banks of this river, we were informed of many interefting fcenes. At Kirkofwal, and Nunnery particularly, the country was reprefented as very engaging; but Corby-caftle, about five miles from Carlifle, was the only place above the town, which we had time to vifit.

At Wetherall we ferried over the river; and landed under the caftle, which ftands on the edge of a lofty bank. This bank ftretches at leaft three miles along the courfe of the river, partly below, but chiefly above the caftle. I give it it's ancient title; tho it is now a mere modern houfe, without the leaft veftige of it's former dignity. Below the caftle, the bank is rocky, and falls precipitately into the water; above, it makes a more gentle defcent; and leaves an edging, which, in fome parts, fpreads into little winding meads, and where it is nar-roweft, is broad enough for a handfome walk. The whole bank, both above, and below the caftle, is covered with wood; large oak, and afh; and in many places the fcenery is rocky alfo. But the rocks are not of the grey kind,

ftained

ftained with a variety of different tints—the *faxa circumlita mufco:* but incline rather to a fandy red, which is not the moft coalefcing hue. They give however great fpirit, and beauty to the fcene.

The bank of the river, *oppofite* to the caftle, is likewife high; in many parts woody; in others affording an intermixture of wood, and lawn. Here ftand the ruins of Wetherall-abbey; tho little more of it is left, than a fquare tower, which is fome ornament, tho no very picturefque one, to the fcene. Thefe ruins were once extenfive, and, I have heard, beautiful; but the dean and chapter of Carlifle, to whom the place belongs, fome years ago carried off the ftones, with more œconomy than tafte, to build a prebendal houfe.

On this fide of the river alfo, an object prefents itfelf, known by the name of *Wetherall-fafeguard,* which is efteemed a great curiofity. It confifts of three chambers cut in the folid rock, which being in this part almoft a precipice, the accefs to the chambers is difficult. It is fuppofed to have been an appendage of the abbey; where the monks, in times of diforder, fecreted their wealth. Some antiquarians fuppofe it to have been inhabited by a

H 4   religious

religious devotee, and call it *St. Conſtantine's cell.* It is rather a curious place, than any great ornament to the ſcene.

To all theſe natural advantages of the ſcenery about Corby-caſtle, the improvements of art have added little. The late proprietor, who had ſeen nothing himſelf; and imagined from the reſort of ſtrangers to ſee the beauty of his ſituation, that they admired his taſte, reſolved to make Corby one of the moſt ſumptuous places in Europe. With this view, he ſcooped his rocks into grottos—fabricated a caſcade, conſiſting of a lofty flight of regular ſtone ſteps —cut a ſtraight walk through his woods, along the banks of the river; at the end of which he reared a temple: and being reſolved to add every ornament, that expence could procure, he hired an artiſt of the country, at four-pence a day (for labour was then cheap) to make ſtatues. Numberleſs were the works of this genius. Diana, Neptune, Polyphemus, Nymphs and Satyrs in abundance, and a variety of other figures, became ſoon the ornaments of the woods; and met the eye of the ſpectator wherever he turned. A punſter, who was re- markable for making only one good pun in his life, made it here. Pointing to one of theſe

ſtrange

ftrange figures, he called it *a fatyr upon the place*.

But the tafte of the prefent age hath deftroyed the pride of the laft. The prefent proprietor hath done little; but what he hath done, is done well. The rocks indeed fcooped into holes, can never be reftored to their native fimplicity, and grandeur. Their bold projections are for ever effaced. Nor could a century reftore thofe trees, which were rooted up to form the vifta. But the ftatues, like the ancient fculpture of the Egyptians, are now no more. The temple is going faft into ruin: and the cafcade (fo frivolous, if it had even been good in it's kind, on the banks of a great, and rapid river) is now overgrown with thickets. The old line of the walk could not eafily be effaced: but a new one, beyond the temple, is carried on, which follows naturally the courfe of the river. And indeed this part of the walk admits more beauty, than any other; for the varieties of ground are greater; the bank, and edging of meadow, are more irregular; and the river more finuous.

This walk having conducted us along the river, through thefe pleafing irregularities, about two miles from the caftle, climbs the

higher

higher grounds, and returns through woods, and beautiful sheep walks, which lie on the sides, and summit of the bank. Through the whole of it, both at the top, and bottom, are many pleasant views; but they are all of the more confined kind.

Many parts of this walk were wrought by the priest of the family, which is a popish branch of the Howards. He belongs to an order, which injoins it's members to manual labour so many hours in the day; laying them, with admirable wisdom, under the *wholesome necessity* of acquiring health, and spirits. I am persuaded that if a studious man were *obliged* to dig three or four hours a day, he would study the better, during the remaining part of it. We had been recommended to the civilities of this ecclesiastic (the family being then in France,) and found him at work in the garden. He received us politely; and discovered the manners of a gentleman, under the garb of a day-labourer, without the least apology for his dress, and occupation. There is something very pleasing in the simplicity and manliness of not being ashamed of the necessary functions of any state, which we have made our option in life.—This

eccle-

ecclefiaftic fucceeded Father Walfh, who has lately engaged the attention of the public.——— I have dwelt the longer on this fcene, as it is the moft admired one in Cumberland.

From Corby-caftle to Warwick, which lies about two miles nearer Carlifle, on the banks of the fame river, the road is beautiful. Many admire the fituation of Warwick alfo. It feems to be a fweet, retired fcene; but we had not time to view it.

The antiquarian's eye is immediately caught here by the parifh-church; the chancel of which, forming the fegment of a circle, and being pierced with fmall lancet-windows, fhews at once, that it is of Norman origin. Tho every other mark were obliterated, he will tell you, that this is 'evidence fufficient of it's antiquity.

SECT.

S E C T.   XXI.

HAVING feen as much of the river Eden, above Carlifle, as our time would allow, we made our next excurfion towards it's mouth, where Brugh-marfh attracted our attention. In our way we had many pleafing river views.

Brugh-marfh lies at the extremity of the Englifh border; running up as far as Solway-frith, which, in this part, divides England from Scotland. It is a vaft extended plain, flat as the furface of a quiet ocean. I do not remember that land, ever gave me before fo vaft an idea of fpace. The idea of this kind, which fuch fcenes as Salifbury-Plain fuggefts, is much lefs pure. The inequality of the ground there, fets bounds to the idea. It is

the

the ocean in a ftorm; in which the idea of
extenfion is greatly broken, and intercepted
by the turbulence of the waves. Brugh-marfh
gives us the idea of folid water, rather than
of land, if we except only the colour :

———————————Intermineable meads,
And vaft favannahs, where the wandering eye
Unfixt, is in a verdant ocean loft.

Brugh-marfh is one of thofe extended plains,
(only more extenfive, than fuch plains commonly are) from which the fea, in a courfe
of ages, hath retired. It is difficult to com-
pute it's limits. It ranges many leagues, in
every direction, from a centre (for fpace fo
diffufe affumes of courfe a circular appearance)
without a hedge, or even a bufh, to inter-
cept it's bounds; till it foften into the azure
mountains of the horizon. Nothing indeed,
but mountains, can circumfcribe fuch a fcene.
All inferior boundaries of wood, and rifing
grounds are loft. On the Englifh fide it is
bounded by that circular chain, in the heart
of Cumberland, in which Skiddaw is pre-
eminent. Nothing intermediate appears. On
the Scotch fide it's courfe is interrupted,
through the fpace of a few leagues, by Solway-
frith;

frith; which spreads, when the tide is at
ebb, into a vast stretch of sand. The plain
however is still preserved. Having passed
this sandy obstruction, it changes it's hue
again into vivid green, and stretches far and
wide into the Scotch border, till it's progress
at length is stopped by the mountains of
Galloway, and Niddsdale. This extension is
as much as the eye can well comprehend.
Had the plain been boundless, like an Arabian
desert, I know not whether it would not have
lost that idea of space, which so vast a circum-
scription gives it.

The whole area of Brugh-marsh, (which
from it's *denomination* we should suppose to
be swampy,) is every where perfectly firm;
and the turf, soft, bright, and pure. Scarce
a weed rears it's head. Nothing appears of
statelier growth than a mushroom, which
spreads here in luxuriant knots.

This vast plain is far from being a desert
waste. Innumerable herds of cattle pasture
at large in it's rich verdure; and range, as in
a state of nature.

But

But tho the primary idea, which this scene reprefents, arifes purely from fpace, and is therefore an idea rather grand than picturefque; yet it is not totally incapable of picturefque embellifhment. It is true, it wants almoft every ingredient of landfcape; on the foreground, it wants objects to preferve the keeping; and in the offskip, that profufion of little parts, which in a fcene of cultivation gives richnefs to diftance. In treating therefore a fubject of this kind on canvas, recourfe muft be had to adventitious objects. Cattle come moft naturally to hand; which being ftationed, in various groups, at different diftances, may ferve both as a foreground to the landfcape, and as a gage to the perfpective.

Brugh-marfh is farther remarkable for having been the fcene of one of the greateft cataftrophes of the Englifh hiftory—the death of Edward the I. Here, after Scotland had made a third attempt to recover it's liberty, that prince, drew together the moft puiffant army, which England had ever feen. The Scots from their borders, faw the plain whitened with tents: but they knew not how

nearly

nearly their deliverance approached. The greateſt events generally arrive unlooked for. They ſaw a delay; and afterwards a confuſion in the mighty hoſt before them: but they heard not, till three days after, that the ſoul and ſpirit of the enterprize was gone; and that their great adverſary lay breathleſs in his camp.

Edward had been taken ill at Carliſle; where he had met his parliament. But neither diſeaſe, nor age (for he was now near ſeventy) could repreſs his ardour. Tho he could not mount his horſe, he ordered himſelf to be carried in a litter to the camp; where his troops received him with acclamations of joy. But it was ſhort-lived. The motion had irritated his diſorder into a violent dyſentery; which immediately carried him off.

The Engliſh borderers long revered the memory of a prince, who had ſo often chaſtiſed an enemy, they hated; and in gratitude reared a pillar to his name; which ſtill teſtifies the ſpot, on which he died. It ſtands rather on the edge of the marſh, and bears this ſimple inſcription.

MEMORIÆ ÆTERNÆ

EDVARDI,

REGIS ANGLIÆ LONGE CLARISSIMI,

QUI, IN BELLI APPARATU

CONTRA SCOTOS OCCUPATUS,

HIC IN CASTRIS OBIIT,

7 JULII A.D. 1307.

Among other places in the neighbourhood of Carlifle, we made an excurfion into Gillsland, with an intention chiefly to fee Naworth-caftle, the vale and ruins of the Abbey of Lanercoft; and the ruins of Scaleby-caftle.

As we leave Carlifle, along the great military road to Newcaftle, the view of the river Eden from Stanwix-bank, is very pleafing. The curve it defcribes; the beautiful meadows it winds through; and the mountains, which clofe the fcene, make all together an amufing combination of objects. Wood only is wanting.

On croffing the river Irthing, about feven
miles from Carlifle, the country, which was
before unpleafing, becomes rich, and interefting.
ing. Here we enter the barony of Gillfland,
an extenfive diftrict, which confifts, in this
part, of a great variety of hill, and dale.
The hills are fandy, bleak, and unpleafant;
but the vallies, which are commonly of the
contracted kind, are beautiful. They are generally woody, and each of them watered by
fome little bufy ftream.—From thefe vallies,
or *gills*, (as the country-people call them,)
with which the whole barony abounds, Camden fuppofes it might poffibly have taken the
name of Gillfland.

On a delightful knoll, gently gliding into
a finuous *gill*, furrounded with full-grown
oak, and overlooking the vale of Lanercoft,
ftands Naworth-caftle. The houfe, which
confifts of two large fquare towers, united
by a main body, is too regular to be beautiful, unlefs thrown into perfpective. It was
formerly one of thofe fortified places, in which

the

the nobility and gentry of the borders were obliged to live, in thofe times of confufion, which preceded the union. And indeed the whole internal contrivance of this caftle appears calculated either to keep an enemy out; or to elude his fearch, if he fhould happen to get in. The idea of a comfortable dwelling is totally excluded. The ftate-rooms are few, and ordinary: but the little apartments, and hiding-holes, acceffible only by dark paffages, and blind ftair-cafes, are innumerable. Many of the clofe receffes, which it contains, are probably at this time, unknown. Nothing indeed can mark in ftronger colours the fears, and jealoufies, and caution of thofe times, than the internal ftruc-ture of one of thefe caftles.

Naworth-caftle was formerly the capital manfion of the barons of Gillfland; who, at fo great a diftance from court, and feated in a country, at that time, untamed by law, are faid to have exercifed very extraordinary powers. The Lord William Howard, who is remembered by the name of *bald Willy*, is ftill the object of invective for his acts of tyranny. His prifons are fhewn; and the fite of his gibbets; where, in the phrafe of

the

the country, he would *head, and hang with-out judge, or jury.*—But it is probable, that his memory is injured. He acted under a standing commiffion of oyer, and terminer from Elizabeth; and was one of thofe bold fpirits, which are neceffary to reprefs the vio-lence of lawlefs times. Many acts of power undoubtedly he committed: but his difficult fituation compelled him. This part of the kingdom was moft harraffed by thofe troops of mifchievous banditti; whom I have juft had occafion to mention. They were a nu-merous, and not an ill-regulated body; act-ing under leaders, whom a fpirit of enter-prize raifed to power. Thefe mifcreants, in times even of profoundeft peace, called for all the warinefs and activity of the chiefs of the country. Sometimes they would plunder in large bodies; and fometimes in little pilfering bands. When they were taken in the fact; or, as it was called, by the *bloody hand,* they were put to inftant death. In other cafes a jury was impannelled.

The active chief, who gave occafion to this digreffion, feems to have lived in as much terror himfelf, as he fpread among others. He had contrived a fort of citadel in his own

I 3   caftle ;

caftle; a room, which is ftill fhewn, with an
iron door, where he conftantly flept, and
where his armour lies rufting to this day.
From him the earls of Carlifle are defcended;
and have been, in fucceffion, the proprietors
of Naworth-caftle.

As we left this old fortrefs, and defcended
the hill towards the ruins of the abbey of
Lanercoft, which lie about two miles farther,
the whole vale, in which they are feated,
opened before us. It is efteemed one of the
moft pleafing fcenes in the country; and indeed we found it fuch. It's area is about half
a mile in breadth, and two or three miles in
length, confifting of one ample fweep. The
fides, which are gentle declivities, are covered
thick with wood, in which larger depreda-
tions have been lately made, than are con-
fiftent with picturefque beauty.—At the diftant
end of the vale, where the woods appear to
unite, the river Irthing enters; which is confiderable enough, tho divided into two channels, to be fully adequate to the fcene.—
The banks of the river, and indeed the whole
area of the vale, are fprinkled with clumps,
and

and fingle trees; which have a good effect in breaking the lines, and regular continuity of the fide-fkreens; and in hiding, here and there, the courfe of, the river; efpecially the bridges, which would otherwife be too bare and formal.

Near that extremity of the vale, which is oppofite to Naworth-caftle, lies the abbey. At a diftance it forms a good object, rifing among the woods. As you approach, it begins to raife a difappointment: and on the fpot, it is but an unpleafing ruin. The whole is a heavy, Saxon pile; compreffed together without any of that airy lightnefs, which accompanies the Gothic. Scarce one *detached* fragment appears in any point of view. The tower is low, and without either form, or ornament; and one of the great ailes is modernized into an awkward parifh-church. The only beautiful part of the whole is the eaft end. It is compofed of four broken ailes; every wall of which confifts of two tiers of arches, affording, a very unufual appearance; and at the fame time a very amufing confufion, from the uncommon multiplication of fo many arches, and pillars.——This part of the abbey feems to have been a feparate

chapel;

chapel; or perhaps an oratory belonging to the noble family of Dacre, which had once poffeffions in thefe parts. Here lie the remains of feveral ancient chiefs of that houfe; whofe fepulchral honours are now almoft intirely obliterated. Their blazoned arms, and Gothic tombs, many of which are fumptuous, are fo matted with briars, and thiftles, that even the foot of curiofity is kept at a diftance.

Except thefe remains of the abbey-church no other parts of this ancient monaftery are now left; but an old gateway; and a fquare building, patched into a farm-houfe, which has no beauty.

In returning to Carlifle we paffed through the valley of Cambeck, which contains fome pleafing fcenery; and a very confiderable Roman ftation, on a high bank at *Caftle-fteeds*.

Rivers often prefent us with very moral analogies; their characters greatly refembling thofe of men. The violent, the reftlefs, the fretful, the active, the fluggifh, the gentle, the bounteous, and many other epithets, belong equally to both. The little ftream,
which

which divides the valley of Cambeck, sug-
gested the analogy. It's whole course is marked
with acts of violence. In every part you see
heaps of barren sand, and gravel, which in
it's furious moods it has thrown up, sometimes on one side, and sometimes on another;
destroying every where the little scenes of
beauty, and plots of cultivation.

About three miles further we visited the
ruins of Scaleby-castle. This was another of
those fortified houses, which are so frequent
in this country.

It stands, as castles rarely do, on a flat;
and yet, tho it's site be ill adapted to any
modes of defence, it has been a place of
more than ordinary strength. Rocks, knolls,
and bold, projecting promontories, on which
castles usually stand, suggest various advantages of situation; and generally determine
the kind of structure. On a flat, the engi-
neer was at liberty to choose his own. Every
part was alike open to assault.

He first drew two circular motes round the
spot he designed to fortify: the circumference
of the outward circle was somewhat more than

half

half a mile. The earth, thrown out of thefe two motes, which were broad and deep, feems to have been heaped up at the centre, where there is a confiderable rife. On this was built the caftle, which was entered by two draw-bridges; and defended by a high tower, and a very lofty wall.

At prefent, one of the motes only remains. The other is filled up; but may ftill be traced. The caftle is more perfect, than fuch build-ings commonly are. The walls are very in-tire; and great part of the tower, which is fquare, is ftill left. It preferved it's perfect form, till the civil wars of the laft century; when the caftle, in too much confidence of it's ftrength, fhut it's gates againft Cromwell, then marching into Scotland; who made it a monument of his vengeance.

What fhare of picturefque genius Crom-well might have, I know not. Certain how-ever it is, that no man, fince Henry the eighth, has contributed more to adorn this country with picturefque ruins. The differ-ence between thefe two mafters lay chiefly in the ftyle of ruins, in which they compofed. Henry adorned his landfcapes with the ruins of abbeys; Cromwell, with thofe of caftles.

I have

I have feen many pieces by this mafter, executed in a very grand ftyle; but feldom a finer monument of his mafterly hand than this. He has rent the tower, and demolifhed two of it's fides; the edges of the other two he has fhattered into broken lines. The chafm difcovers the whole plan of the internal ftructure—the veftiges of the feveral ftories—the infertion of the arches, which fupported them —the windows for fpeculation; and the breaft-work for affault.

The walls of this caftle are uncommonly magnificent. They are not only of great height, but of great thicknefs; and defended by a large baftion; which appears to be of more modern workmanfhip. The greateft part of them is chambered within, and wrought into fecret receffes. A maffy portcullis gate leads to the ruins of what was once the habitable part of the caftle, in which a large vaulted hall is the moft remarkable apartment; and under it, are dark, and capacious dungeons.

The area within the mote, which confifts of feveral acres, was originally intended to fupport the cattle, which fhould be driven thither in times of alarm. When the houfe

was

was inhabited (whose chearful and better days are still remembered, this area was the garden; and all around, on the outside of the mote stood noble trees, irregularly planted, the growth of a century. Beneath the trees ran a walk round the castle; to which the situation naturally gave that pleasing curve, which in modern days hath been so much the object of art. This walk might admit of great embellishment. On one hand, it commands the ruins of the castle in every point of view; on the other, a country, which tho flat, is not unpleasing; consisting of extensive meadows, (which a little planting might turn into beautiful lawns,) bounded by lofty mountains.

This venerable pile has now undergone a second ruin. The old oaks and elms, the ancient natives of the scene, are felled. Weeds, and spiry grass have taken possession of the courts, and obliterated the very plan of a garden: while the house itself, (whose hospitable roof deserved a better fate,) is now a scene of desolation. Two wretched families, the only inhabitants of the place, occupied the two ends of the vaulted hall, when we saw it, the fragment of a tattered curtain, reaching

half

half way to the top, being the fimple boundary of their refpective limits. All the reft
was wafte: no other part of the houfe was
habitable. The chambers unwindowed, and
almoft unroofed, fluttered with rags of ancient tapeftry, were the haunt of daws, and
pigeons; which burft out in clouds of duft,
when the doors were opened: while the floors,
yielding to the tread, made curiofity dangerous.
A few pictures, heir-looms of the wall, which
have long deferved oblivion, by I know not
what fate, were the only appendages of this
diffolving pile, which had triumphed over the
injuries of time.

Shakefpear's caftle of Macbeth could not
have been more the haunt of fwallows and
martins, than this. We faw them every
where about the ruins; either twittering on
broken coins; threading fome fractured arch;
or purfuing each other, in fcreaming circles,
round the walls of the caftle.*

---

* In this old caftle the author of this tour was born,
and fpent his early youth; which muft be his apology for
dwelling fo long upon it.——Since this defcription was written, it has, in fome degree, been repaired.

SECT.

S E C T. XXII.

OUR laſt expedition, in the neighbourhood of Carliſle, was to ſee the improvements of Mr. Graham of Netherby; and the ſcene of deſolation, occaſioned by the late overflowing of Solway-moſs.

Mr. Graham's improvements are not con-fined to a garden, or the ſpace of a mile or two around his houſe. The whole country is changed; and from a barren waſte, hath aſſumed the face—if not of beauty, at leaſt of fertility.

The domain of Netherby lies on the very ſkirts of the Engliſh border. The Romans conſidered it as a part of Caledonia; and ſhut it from the Britiſh pale. In after ages the diſtrict around it aſſumed the name of the

Debate-

Debateable-land, and was the great rendezvous of thofe crews of outlawed banditti, who,
under the denomination of *Mofs-troopers*, plun-
dered the country. We have already had
occafion to mention them. In this neighbourhood were the ftrong holds of many of their
chiefs; particularly of Johnny Armftrong of
famous memory; the moted ruins of whofe
caftle are ftill extant.

Among thefe people the arts of tillage were
unknown. It was abfurd to be at the trouble
of fowing land themfelves, when they could
fo eafily plunder the lands of others.

Tho the union of the two kingdoms put
an end to the ravages on the borders; yet the
manners of the inhabitants, in fome refpects,
fuffered little change. Their native lazinefs,
and inattention to all the arts of hufbandry,
remained. They occupied large tracts of excellent land at eafy rates: but having no idea
of producing yearly crops from the fame foil by
culture; they ploughed their patches of ground
alternately, leaving them to recover their fertility by fallows. An indolent and fcanty
maintenance was all they wifhed; and this they
obtained from a fmall portion of their land,
with a fmall portion of their labour. Their

lords

lords in the mean time, never lived on the spot; and knew little of the state either of the country, or of it's inhabitants.

Mr. Graham immediately set himself to alter this state of things. He built a noble mansion for himself; which makes a grand appearance, rising on the ruins of a Roman station. Without the presence of the lord, he knew it was in vain to expect reformation. He divided his lands into moderate farms; and built commodious farm-houses. As his lands improved, he raised his rents: and his tenants in proportion found it necessary to increase their labour. Thus he has doubled his own income, and introduced a spirit of industry into the country. These indolent inhabitants of the borders begin now to work like other labourers; and notwithstanding they pay higher rents, live more comfortably: for idleness can never be attended with the comforts of industry.

To bring about this great change, Mr. Graham thinks it necessary to rule his subjects with a rod of iron. While he makes them labourers, he keeps them slaves.—Perhaps indeed the rough manners of the people in those parts, could not easily be moulded by the hand of tenderness.

The feudal idea of vaſſalage, which has long diſappeared in all the internal parts of England, remains here in great force; and throws a large ſhare of power into the hands of the landholder. Mr. Graham's eſtates, which are very extenſive, contain about ſix hundred tenants; all of whom, with their families, lie in a manner at his mercy for their ſubſiſtence. Their time and labour he commands, by their mode of tenure, whenever he pleaſes. Under the denomination of *boon-days*, he expects, at any time, their perſonal ſervice; and can, in a few hours, muſter the ſtrength of five or ſix hundred men and horſes.

Once he had occaſion to call them together on military ſervice. On a ſuppoſed injury,* which, about two years ago, he had done the Scotch borderers by intercepting the ſalmon in the Eſk, a body of three hundred of theſe people marched down upon him with an intention to deſtroy his works. He had intelligence of their deſign, and iſſuing his precepts,

---

* I have heard ſince, that this injury has been proved to be a real one; and that reparation hath been made.

muſtered,

muftered, in a few hours, above four hundred
men before his gates, armed as the exigence
would allow: and if the Scotch, on finding
fuch fuperiority, had not retreated; Mr. Graham, who told us the ftory himfelf, faid he
believed, that all the fpirit and animofity of
ancient times would have revived on this
occafion.

In a civil light he acts on as large a fcale.
His manor-courts are kept with great ftrict-
nefs; in which his attorney, with a jury, fits
regularly to try caufes; and the tenants are
injoined, at the hazard of being turned out of
their farms, to bring into thefe courts every
fuit under the value of five pounds. Thus he
prevents much ill-blood among them, by bringing their difputes to a fpeedy iffue; and giving
the quarrel no time to rankle. He faves them
alfo much expence: for a fuit, which in the
king's courts would at leaft coft five or fix
pounds; may in his, be carried through all it's
forms for eight-pence.—At Patterdale we found
a nominal king. Here we found almoft a king
in reality.

The works on the Efk, which gave fo much
offence to the Scotch borderers, deferve more
notice. They confifted of a maffy head thrown

K 2   acrofs

acrofs the river, conftructed, at a great expence, of hewn ftone. This mole was formed
at right angles with the bank; but the floods
of the enfuing winter fwept it away. It was
attempted a fecond time on the fame plan; but
was a fecond time deftroyed. Mr. Brindley
was then fent for, whofe works near Manchef-
ter had given him fo high a reputation. He
changed the plan; and inftead of carrying the
mole in a direct line acrofs the river, formed it
in a curve, arching againft the ftream : fo that
it refifts the current, as a bridge does the
incumbent weight. This work has ftood
feveral very great floods, and feems fufficiently
firm.* From the curvature of it's form the
fall of the water appears alfo to more advantage. It now forms a femi-circular cafcade,
which has a good effect.

The chief end which this work had in view,
was a fifhery. At this place falmon coops

---

* Since this was written, I am informed, Mr. Brindley's
work was deftroyed from an unfufpected quarter, when the
water was low. On the breaking of a froft, a great quantity of ice coming down the river, and collecting at this
ftoppage, fome of it edged under the loofer parts of the foundation, and being preffed on with a continued acceffion of
ftrength, acted like a wedge, and the whole blew up.

are

are placed; where all the fiſh, which enter
the Eſk, are taken. But beſides this, and
other purpoſes of utility, it adds great beauty
to the neighbourhood. The Eſk, which was
before in compariſon, a ſhallow ſtream, gliding
unſeen beneath it's banks, is now a noble
piece of water, raiſed to a level with them,
and ſeen to great advantage from the houſe,
and every part of the ground.

It was in this part of the country where, that
dreadful inundation, over-flowing from the
Solway-moſs, deſtroyed lately ſo large a diſtrict.
To ſee the effects of this, was the object of
our next expedition.

Solway-moſs is a flat area, about ſeven
miles in circumference. The *ſubſtance* of it
is a groſs fluid, compoſed of mud, and the
putrid fibres of heath, diluted by internal
ſprings, which ariſe in every part. The *ſurface* is a dry cruſt, covered with moſs, and
ruſhes; offering a fair appearance over an
unſound bottom—ſhaking under the leaſt preſ-
ſure. Cattle by inſtinct know, and avoid it.
Where ruſhes grow, the bottom is foundeſt.
The adventrous paſſenger therefore, who ſome-

times,

times, in dry feafons, traverfes this perilous
wafte to fave a few miles, picks his cautious
way over the rufhy tuffocks, as they appear
before him. If his foot flip, or if he venture
to defert this mark of fecurity, it is poffible he
may never more be heard of.

At the battle of Solway, in the time of
Henry VIII. Oliver Sinclair was imprudently
fet over the Scotch army, which had no confidence in him. A total rout enfued; when an
unfortunate troop of horfe, driven by their
fears, plunged into this morafs, which inftantly clofed upon them. The tale, which
was traditional; was generally believed; but
is now authenticated. A man and horfe in
compleat armour were lately found by the
peat-diggers, in the place, where it was always
fuppofed the affair had happened; and are
preferved at the houfe of a Scotch baronet, if
I miftake not, of the name of Maxwell; as
we were informed by a gentleman * of the
borders, who affured us he had feen them
himfelf. The fkeleton of each was well preferved; and the different parts of the armour
eafily diftinguifhed.

---

* Jofeph Dacre, Efq, of Kirklinton, near Longtown.

Solway-mofs is bounded on the fouth by a cultivated, and well-inhabited plain, which declines gently, through the fpace of a mile, to the river Efk. This plain is rather lower than the mofs itfelf, being feparated from it by a breaftwork formed by digging peat, which makes an irregular, low, perpendicular, line of black boundary.

It was the burfting of the mofs through this peat breaftwork, over the plain between it and the Efk, which occafioned that dreadful ruin, which we came hither to explore. ———The more remarkable circumftances, relating to this calamitous event, as we had them on the beft authority, were thefe.

On the 16th of november, 1771, in a dark, tempeftuous night, the inhabitants of the plain were alarmed with a dreadful crafh, which they could in no way account for. Many of them were then abroad in the fields, watching their cattle; left the Efk, which was rifing violently in the ftorm, fhould carry them off. None of thefe miferable people could conceive the noife they heard to proceed from any caufe, but the overflowing of the river in fome fhape, tho to them unaccountable. Such indeed, as lived nearer the fource of the eruption, were
fenfible,

fenfible, that the noife came in a different direction; but were equally at a lofs for the caufe.

In the mean time the enormous mafs of fluid fubftance, which had burft from the mofs, moved flowly on, fpreading itfelf more and more, as it got poffeffion of the plain. Some of the inhabitants, through the terror of the night, could plainly difcover it advancing, like a moving hill. This was in fact the cafe; for the gufh of mud carried before it, through the firft two or three hundred yards of it's courfe, a part of the breaftwork; which, tho low, was yet feveral feet in perpendicular height. But it foon depofited this folid mafs; and became a heavy fluid. One houfe after another, it fpread round—filled—and crufhed into ruin; juft giving time to the terrified inhabitants to efcape. Scarce any thing was faved; except their lives: nothing of their furniture: few of their cattle. Some people were even furprized in their beds, and had the additional diftrefs of flying naked for fafety.

The morning-light explained the caufe of this amazing fcene of terror; and fhewed the calamity in it's full extent: and yet, among all the conjectures of that dreadful night, the

mifchief

mifchief which really happened, had never
been fuppofed. Who could have imagined,
that a breaftwork, which had ftood for ages,
fhould give way? or that thofe fubterraneous
floods, which had been bedded in darknefs,
fince the memory of man, fhould burft from
their black abode?

This dreadful inundation, tho the firft fhock
of it was the moft tremendous, continued ftill
fpreading for many weeks, till it covered the
whole plain—an area of five hundred acres;
and, like molten metal poured into a mould,
filled all the hollows, lying in fome parts
thirty or forty feet deep, reducing the whole
to one level furface. The overplus found it's
way into the Efk; where it's quantity was
fuch, as to annoy the fifh; no falmon, during
that feafon, venturing into the river. We
were affured alfo, that many lumps of earth,
which had floated out at fea, were taken up,
fome months after, at the ifle of Man.

As we defcended from the higher grounds
to take a nearer view of this fcene of horror,
it exhibited a very grand appearance. The
whole plain was covered by a thick fmoke,

occa-

occafioned by a fmothering fire fet to it in various parts, with a view to confume it; and brought before us that fimple, and fublime idea of *the fmoke of a country going up like the fmoke of a furnace.*

When we came to the plain on that fide, which is next the Efk, it had fo forbidding an afpect, as far as we could difcover through the fmoke, that we almoft defpaired of croffing to the chafm, as we had intended. On horfeback it was impoffible; and when we had alighted, we ftood hefitating on the brink, whether it were prudent, even on foot, to attempt fo dangerous a march.

While we remained in this fituation, we obferved feveral groups of peafants working in the ruins: and beckoning to the neareft, one of the group came forward. He was an elderly man, ftrengthening his fteps with a long meafuring wand. His features, and gait, tho hard and clownifh, were marked with an air of vulgar confequence. As he approached, one of our company, who knew him, accofted him by the name of Wilfon; and we found he was the perfon who conducted the works which were fet on foot to clear the foil of this melancholy incumbrance.

On

On informing him of our difficulties, and
afking, whether we might venture acrofs the
plain; he bad us, like Cæfar, with an air of
affurance, follow him, and fear nothing.
From one tuffock to another we followed,
fometimes ftepping—fometimes leaping—and
fometimes hefitating, whether to go on, or to
return. In very difficult places our guide
condefcended to lay us a plank. In the midft
of our perplexity, one of our company, ftray-
ing a ftep from the right path, fell in; but
the mud being fhallow in that part, he fank
only to the knees. Mr. Wilfon helped him
out; but reprimanded his careleffnefs. The
reproof and the example having a good effect
upon us all, we followed our guide, like pack-
horfes in a ftring, and at length compleated
our undertaking.

When we got to the gulph, from whence
all this mifchief had iffued, the fpectacle was
hideous. The furface of *the mafs itfelf* had
fuffered little change. Near the chafm it
appeared indented, through a fpace of feveral
yards: but not in any degree as one would
have expected from fo vaft a difcharge. The
mouth of the chafm was heaped round with
monftrous piles of ruin, formed by the broken

breaftbreaſtwork, and ſhell of the moſs, on the firſt great burſt; and a black, moſſy tinĉture continued ſtill to iſſue from it. If this continue to run, as it probably will, it may be a fortunate circumſtance; and ſave the country from any farther miſchief, by draining this bloated maſs through a perpetual diſcharge.

As we ſtood on the higher ground, and got to windward of the ſmoke, we obtained a clear idea of the plain, and of the courſe of the irruption over it. Many fragments of a very large ſize, which had been carried away in the firſt full ſtream of the diſcharge, appeared thrown to a conſiderable diſtance. Theſe were what made that moving bulwark, which ſome of the inhabitants had ſeen in the night. Fragments of a ſmaller ſize, (and yet many of theſe conſiderable) appeared ſcattered over the plain, as the heavy torrent was able to carry them. The interſtices between the fragments, which had been filled with fluid moſs, were now baked by the heat of the ſun, and cruſted over like the great ſurface of the moſs itſelf. Here and there, along this ſurface, the broken rafters of a houſe, or the top of a blaſted tree were ſeen; and made an odd appearance, riſing as it were, out of the ground, in which they

were

were half funk. But through the whole wafte, there was not the leaft fign left of any culture; tho this plain had once been the pride of the country: Lands, which in the evening would have let for twenty fhillings an acre, by the morning-light were not worth fix-pence.

On this well cultivated plain twenty-eight families had their dwellings, and little farms; every one of which, except a few, who lived near the fkirts of it, had the world totally to begin again. Mr. Graham, agreeably to the prudential maxims he has ever obferved, affords them little affiftance himfelf; and difcourages the bounty of others. He feems to wifh his dominions fhould thrive by induftry alone; and would have his fubjects depend on this great virtue for the fupply of every want, and the reparation of every lofs. If the maxim, in fo full an extent, be good; it requires at leaft, a great hardinefs of refolution to carry it into practice.

Whether the immenfe work of clearing this plain can ever totally be effected, is a doubt with many. It is attempted however with great fpirit, through the united force of the two powerful elements of fire and water.

All

All the skirts, and other parts of it which are drier than the rest, are reduced by fire; which occasioned the great smoke from the plain, as we descended into it; and which, at that distance, appeared to arise from the whole area.

But this method is not found very effectual; as it reaches only a little below the surface. Much more is expected from the application of water; which is the part our guide Mr. Wilson has undertaken.—How well qualified he is for the undertaking, and in what manner he proposes to accomplish it, may be conceived from the following story.

Mr. Graham's house stands on an eminence, with higher grounds above it. A little on one fide of the front, stood a knoll, which made a disagreeable appearance before his windows.— Being desirous therefore of removing it, he sent to Newcastle for a person accustomed to works of this kind. The undertaker came, surveyed the ground, and estimated the expence of moving fo much earth, at thirteen hundred pounds.

While

While the affair was in agitation, Mr. Graham heard, that Wilson had said, the earth might be removed at a much easier rate. He was examined on the subject; and his answers appeared so rational, that he was set to work. He had already surveyed the higher grounds, where he first collected all the springs he found, into two large reservoirs; from which he cut a precipitate channel, pointed at an abrupt corner of the knoll. He cut also a channel of communication between his two reservoirs. These being both filled, he opened his sluices, and let out such a continued torrent of water, (the upper pool feeding the lower) that he very soon carried away the corner of the knoll, against which he had pointed his artillery. He then charged again, and levelled against another part with equal success. In short, by a few efforts of this kind, he carried away the whole hill; and told Mr. Graham, with an air of triumph, that, if he pleased, he would carry away his house next. The work was compleated in a few days; and Mr. Graham himself informed us, that the whole expence did not amount to twenty pounds.

This man, with so much genius about him, lives in the lowest stile of life; and works for

the

the loweft wages. When we regretted, that
he was paid fo inadequately to his worth, we
were affured, as his appearance indeed teftified,
that he had no higher idea of happinefs, than
to get drunk after his day's labour: and that
better wages would only deftroy him fooner. -

I have fince heard, that one hundred and
fifty acres of the plain are now cleared by the
ingenuity of this man: and that there is reafon
to believe, he will in time ftill clear a more
confiderable part. From a refervoir formed
by a little ftream at the higheft part of the
overflowed ground, he cut channels in various
directions to the Efk: and when the water was
let off, he placed numbers of men by the fide
of each ftream, who rolled into it large maffes
of moffy earth, which had been hardened by
the fun. The ftream tumbled them into the
river; and the river conveyed them to the
fea.

SECT.

S E C T. XXIII.

HAVING feen fuch parts of the country on the borders of England, as were moft curious; we fet out on our return. But inftead of taking the Kefwick-road, we propofed to vary our rout by the mountains of Brugh.*

At Penrith the road divides. We turned to the left, towards Appelby; and foon fell into a rich, and beautiful vale, in which the river Lowther, gliding under lofty woody banks, bore us company a confiderable way.

When we croffed that river, the fituation of Brougham-caftle, one of the feats of the

---

* See page 168. Vol. I.

L   celebrated

celebrated countefs of Pembroke, attracted our notice. It had not efcaped the notice of the Romans; who fixed here a ftation to command the country. It appears as great, at this time, in a picturefque light, as it did formerly in a military one. But we had not time to ride up to it; contenting ourfelves with viewing it only as the ornament of a fecond diftance.

At Clifton the road opens again into a wild fcene. Here we examined the fpot, where, in the year 1745, the rebels entering an inclofed country, made a ftand; and lined the hedges to retard the duke of Cumberland's purfuit. Sir Jofeph York, in his road from Ireland, had been there, we found, a few days before. He had accompanied the duke in his expedition againft the rebels; and ftopped at Clifton to review the fcene. He left the people, we were informed, much pleafed with his remembering a gallant action, which had been achieved, about that time, by a heroine of the country, who had carried a letter acrofs the fire of the rebels, when no other meffenger could be obtained.

. From

From Clifton, we turned afide to fee Low-ther-hall, the feat of fir James Lowther. It is only a temporary houfe, the old manfion having been burnt in the time of the late lord Lonfdale. But materials are now colleſting for a grand ſtruſture. It is ſituated in an ex-tenſive park, which contains a great variety of beautiful fcenery.

From Lowther-hall we purfued our rout to Appelby, keeping on our left that vaſt traſt of barren country, called Wingfield-foreſt.

The ſituation of Appelby-caſtle, which be-longs to the earl of Thanet, is magnificent. It ſtands. on a rocky eminence, falling preci-pitately into the river Eden; which half in-circles it. The banks of the river, and the fides of the precipice, are finely hung with wood. The caſtle is ſtill in good repair; and is a noble pile. But, in a piſturefque light, it lofes half it's beauty, from it's being broken into two parts. A *fmaller* break from a grand pile removes heavinefs; and is a fource

of

of beauty. We have feen the principle exemplified in mountains, and other objects.*
But here the whole is divided into two parts,
of fuch *equal* dimenfions, that each afpires
to pre-eminence. Each therefore becomes a
feparate whole: and both together diftract
the eye. The detached part fhould always
obferve a due inferiority. But what is faid of
thefe two detached parts of the caftle, is meant
only with regard to that view of it, which
appears *from the road*. If you go *round it,*
you are prefented with other views, in which
it is feen more advantageoufly; particularly
where you fee the bridge, and the firft opening into the vale of Eden. There the caftle
takes a very grand fituation on a hanging
rock over the river; and the *detached part*
makes but an *inconfiderable* appearance.

We had not time to take a view *from* the
caftle; which muft command a beautiful diftance, over the vale.

Appelby-caftle was the Apallaba of the
Romans; and preferves it's origin clearer in
it's etymology, than the generality of Roman
ftations.

---

* See page 55, Vol. II.

This

This caftle was formerly the favourite manfion of Ann, countefs of Pembroke, Dorfet,
and Montgomery. As this very extraordinary
lady is ftill the object of great veneration in
thefe parts: as her hiftory is curious, and lefs
known than it ought to be; and as it is fo
intimately connected with all this country;
I thought the following digreffion a proper
one.

She was the daughter of George Clifford,
earl of Cumberland; one of the heroes of the
gallant age of Elizabeth. This noble perfon
diftinguifhed himfelf chiefly by his naval ex-
peditions; on which he was fuffered, in thofe
frugal times, to expend a great portion of
his patrimony. In return for his patriotifm,
he was appointed by his royal miftrefs, her
champion in all tilts and tournaments; where
the grace, and dignity of his behaviour, and
his fkill and addrefs in arms, were equally
admired. The rich armour he wore, on
thefe occafions, is ftill fhewn in this caftle.

Lady Ann Clifford was only ten years of
age, when her father died. But her education was conducted by two excellent women—

her

her mother, a daughter of the earl of Bedford—
and afterwards by her aunt the countess of
Warwick.

In her early youth she married lord Buck-
hurst, earl of Dorset; with whom during a
few years she lived very happily. But he
soon leaving her a widow; she married, six
years after, Philip earl of Pembroke, and
Montgomery.

This nobleman, through the favour of
James I. possessed, as a reward for his great
skill in the arts of hunting, and hawking,
a prodigious estate; not less, at that time,
than eighteen thousand pounds a year. His
manner of living was sumptuous beyond example; and his apparatus for field-sports
magnificent beyond belief. His dog-kennels
were superb; and his stables vied with pa-
laces. But his falconry was his chief pride;
which he had furnished, at a wonderful expence, with birds of game; and proper per-
sons to manage, train and exercise them.

Here ends the history of Philip earl of
Pembroke—unless we add, that in private
life, he was vicious, ignorant, and unlettered
in a surprizing degree; and that in public,
his character was stained with ingratitude, and

tergiver-

tergiverfation, by the noble hiftorian of thofe unfortunate times.

With this worthlefs man his unhappy lady lived near twenty years. During the latter part of his life indeed he became fo diffolute, that fhe was obliged to leave him.

About the time of his death fhe found her-felf poffeffed of a very ample fortune. For, it feems, her immediate fucceffion to the large eftates of her anceftors in the north, had been difputed by an uncle, who inherited the title : and an award had been given againft her by James I. to which however fhe would not fubmit. But the uncle, and his fon both dying, the great eftates of the Cliffords, tho confiderably impaired by her father's generofity, came to her without any farther moleftation. She had befides two large jointures. That which fhe received from her firft hufband, was between three, and four thoufand, a year; and that from the earl of Pembroke was nearly equal to it.

On the event of the earl of Pembroke's death, fhe immediately laid out the whole plan of her future life ; determining to retire into the north ; and fpend it on her own eftate.

In ancient times the earls of Cumberland
poffeffed five noble caftles in the three counties of Yorkfhire, Weftmoreland, and Cumberland——Skipton—Pendragon—Appelby—
Brougham—and Brugh. The tower of Bar-
don alfo was another fortified feat, where
they fometimes refided. But all thefe caftles
had fuffered in the late civil wars; and were
reduced, more or lefs, to a ftate of great decay.

The countefs of Pembroke however determined, on her coming into the north, to
repair and furnifh them all. This great
work fhe compleated during the years 1657,
and 1658; and placed over the gate of each
caftle the following infcription:

THIS CASTLE WAS REPAIRED BY THE LADY
ANN CLIFFORD, COUNTESS DOWAGER OF PEM-
BROKE, &c. IN THE YEAR —— AFTER THE MAIN
PART OF IT HAD LAIN RUINOUS EVER SINCE
1648, WHEN IT WAS DEMOLISHED, ALMOST TO
THE GROUND BY THE PARLIAMENT THEN SIT-
TING AT WESTMINSTER, BECAUSE IT HAD BEEN
A GARRISON IN THE CIVIL WARS. IS. LVIII. 12.
LAUS DEO!

Oliver Cromwell was, at this time, at the
head of affairs; whofe hypocrify and villany
the countefs of Pembroke detefted: and as
fhe

she had too much spirit to conceal her sentiments, it is probable, the protector was enough informed, how little she esteemed him. Her friends therefore, knowing the jealousy of his temper, advised her not to be so profuse in building; as they were well assured, that as soon as she had built her castles, he would order them to be destroyed. But she answered with great spirit, "Let him destroy them if he will: but he shall surely find, that as often as he destroys them, I will rebuild them, while he leaves me a shilling in my pocket."

She shewed her contempt for Cromwell, and her own high spirit, on another occasion. Her uncle had left her affairs so involved, that she found herself under a necessity of recovering some of her rights by a tedious lawsuit. The affair being represented to Cromwell by the opposite party, he offered his mediation. But she answered loftily, she would never accept it, while there was any law to be found in England. "What! said she, does he imagine, that I, who refused to submit to king James, will submit to him?"

But

But notwithftanding her fpirit, neither her caftles, nor her eftates were injured. Some afcribed this lenity to Cromwell's reverence of her virtue; which is very improbable: others, to her numerous friends, with whom the protector wifhed to keep fair; which, it is moft likely, was the truth.

Her diflike to Cromwell was not founded on party; but on principle. She had the fame diflike afterwards to Charles, when fhe became acquainted with the fpirit of his government. On being preffed by her friends, fometime after the reftoration, to go to court; " By no means, faid fhe; unlefs I may be allowed to wear blinkers."*

Befides her caftles, fhe found likewife in ruins, almoft all the churches, belonging to the feveral villages on her eftates. The fpire of one had been beaten down: another had been turned into a magazine: a third into a hofpital. Seven of them were in this ruinous condition: each of which fhe either built from the ground, or repaired; furnifh-

---

* Blinkers are thofe blinds affixed to the bridles of coach-horfes, which prevent their feeing what they ought not to fee.

ing

ing them all with decent pews; that her tenants, in every part of her eftates, might have churches in their neighbourhood.

Her feveral buildings, and repairs, at her firft coming into the north, did not coft her lefs, than forty thoufand pounds.

At each of her caftles fhe refided a part of every year; regularly moving from one to the other; over-looking the whole of her vaft eftates; and blefling the country, wherever fhe went. She was every where the common patronefs of all, who were diftreffed. Her heart was as large, as her ability: and mifery of every kind, that could get it's ftory fairly reprefented to her, was fure of relief.

Nor was fhe content with *occafional* acts of charity; but made many of her charitable intentions *permanent* by endowments. The greateft of thefe works were two hofpitals, which fhe founded.

One little pleafing monument of this kind ftands by the fide of the road, between Penrith and Appelby. It is a monument indeed rather of her filial piety, than of her charity. On this fpot, in her early youth, fhe had parted with her beloved mother; whom fhe never afterwards faw. She always remembered

bered this parting-fcene with the tendereft feelings; and, when fhe came to refide in Weftmoreland, fhe raifed, among her other buildings a pillar to record it; with a ftone-table at it's bafe. The pillar, which is ftill known in the country by the name of *Countefs-pillar*, is decorated with her arms; a fun-dial, for the benefit of travellers; and the following infcription.

THIS PILLAR WAS ERECTED IN THE YEAR 1656, BY ANN COUNTESS DOWAGER OF PEM-BROKE, &c. FOR A MEMORIAL OF HER LAST PARTING, IN THIS PLACE, WITH HER GOOD AND PIOUS MOTHER, MARGARET, COUNTESS DOWAGER OF CUMBERLAND, ON THE 2d OF APRIL 1616: IN MEMORY WHEREOF SHE HATH LEFT AN ANNUITY OF £4. TO BE DISTRIBUTED TO THE POOR OF THE PARISH OF BROUGHAM, EVERY 2d DAY OF APRIL FOR EVER, UPON THE STONE-TABLE PLACED HARD BY. LAUS DEO!

Her very houfe-hold was a noble charity. Her fervants were generally the children of her tenants; and were fure of a provifion, if they behaved well. Her women-fervants had always little portions given them, to begin the world with, if they married to pleafe her.

The

The calamities of the times alfo, during Cromwell's government, particularly the diftreffed fituation of feveral ejected minifters of the church, furnifhed her with ample opportunities of exerting her generofity. Among others, fhe was particularly kind to King, afterwards bifhop of Chichefter; and Duppa, and Morley, both afterwards bifhops of Winchefter. To each of thefe fhe allowed £40. a year; and when, in their diftreffes abroad, they informed her, that a fum of money would be of more fervice to them, than the annuities fhe was pleafed to give them; fhe remitted a thoufand pounds to be divided among them.

She was a lady of uncommon prudence in the management of her affairs. Bifhop Rainbow fums up her character on this head, in two words, by calling her a perfect miftrefs of *forecaft*, and *aftercaft*.

For the numberlefs acts of bounty, that flowed from her, fhe depended, under God, on two things—her regularity in keeping accounts; and her great economy.

With regard to the former, in whatever caftle fhe refided, an office was kept, in which all her receipts, and difburfements were entered
tered

tered with commercial exactnefs. Of her private charities, fhe kept an account herfelf: but was fo regular, that, at any time by comparing it with her public accounts, fhe had, at once, a compleat view of the fituation of her affairs.

Her economy was equal to her exactnefs. Nothing was fpent in vanity. Nothing was trifled away. All her family-expences were under the article of neceffaries: and the very form of regularity, in which they conftantly ran, made one year a check upon another.

The fpirit, which fhe fhewed in defending her rights, may perhaps be mentioned alfo among her plans of economy. It was a fpirit not often exerted; but when it was raifed, it always carried her vigoroufly to the end of the queftion; and, no doubt, fecured her from many contentions, which might otherwife have difturbed her, in the midft of fo complex a property; and in thofe dubious days, when legal rights were fo much unhinged. I have mentioned her fpirit, in one fuit, with regard to an affair of confequence. We have an account of another, tho of lefs importance.

It

It was a cuſtom, on all her eſtates, for each tenant to pay, beſides his rent, an annual *boon-ben*, as it was called. This had ever been acknowledged a juſt claim; and is, I believe, to this day, paid on many of the great eſtates in the north; being generally conſidered as a ſteward's perquiſite.

It happened, that a rich clothier from Halifax, one Murgatroyd, having taken a tenement near Skipton, was called on by the ſteward of the caſtle for his *boon-ben*. On his refuſal to pay it, the counteſs ordered a ſuit to be commenced againſt him. He was obſtinate; and ſhe determined; ſo it was carried into length. At laſt ſhe recovered her hen; but at the expence of £200.——It is ſaid, that after the affair was decided, ſhe invited Mr. Murgatroyd to dinner; and drawing the hen to her, which was ſerved up as the firſt diſh, "Come, ſaid ſhe, Mr. Murgatroyd, let us now be good friends? ſince you allow the hen to be dreſſed at my table, we'll divide it between us."

She had a mind improved, and cultivated in many parts of learning. Dr. Donn, in his humorous manner, uſed to ſay, *ſhe knew how to converſe of every thing; from predeſtination*

nation to flea-filk. But hiftory feems to have been her chief amufement; to the ftudy of which fhe was probably firft led, by examining the hiftory of her own anceftors. This indeed comprehended, in a great degree, the hiftory of England from the times of the conqueft: for there were few fcenes of public life, in which her progenitors, the Veteriponts and the Cliffords, an active race of men, were not deeply engaged.

She feems to have entertained a defign of collecting materials for a hiftory of thefe two potent northern families. At a great expence fhe employed learned men to make collections, for this purpofe, from the records in the tower; the rolls; and other depofitaries of public papers; which being all fairly tranfcribed, filled three large volumes. This work, which contains anecdotes of a great variety of original characters, exerting themfelves on very important occafions, is ftill, I have heard, among the family-records at Appelby-caftle.

While fhe was thus careful to preferve the honour of her anceftors; fhe inftituted a very

---

* A kind of raw filk ufed, at that time, in embroidery.

fevere

severe historical restraint, if I may so call it, on herself. In a large folio volume, which made a part of her equipage, when she travelled from one castle to another, she ordered an entry to be made, under her own inspection, of the transactions of every day. To what particulars this journal extended, I have not learned. But if it was kept, as it probably was, by a confidential secretary, it might have included very minute particulars. What an interesting collection of valuable anecdotes might be furnished from the incidents of such a life! What a satyr would it be on the vanity, the dissipation, and frivolous employments of the generality of the great! This work, I am informed, is still extant; and in the hands of the earl of Thanet.*

But the most conspicuous part of the character of this illustrious lady, was her piety, and great attachment to religion. No doubt the amiable instructors of her youth had given her disposition, naturally serious, a proper

---

* I have since been informed, that the late earl of Thanet destroyed it, as it contained many severe remarks on several characters of those times, which the earl supposed might give offence to their families.

M   direction:

direction: but perhaps the best school, in which she had learned to think justly, was, that school of affliction, the house of her second husband, the earl of Pembroke; whose dissipated, abandoned life had taught her, more than any thing else, the vanity of all earthly things, unless used for the purposes they were given.

Few divines were better versed in scripture, than she was. She could quote it pertinently on all occasions; and never failed to read a portion of it every day; or have it read to her, in the latter part of her life.

The new testament was her principal study. Next to it she was particularly fond of the psalms of David; and had those appointed for the day, read regularly to her.

She had been bred up in the church of England from her youth; and tho she could not, in the fanatical times of the usurpation, attend any public service; yet in the worst of those times she never failed to hear the church-service in her own private chapels, which she had been careful to fit up in all her castles. Many menaces of sequestrations she recived from the ruling powers, if she persisted in that practice. But she shewed the same spirit on this occasion, which she had

had before fhewn on many others. She continued her practice; and left them to do
as they pleafed. No attempts however were
made againft her.

' She had no idea of pomp, and grandeur.
With regard to herfelf, her mode of living
was rather parfimonious.' Amidft all the objects of her generofity, herfelf was the only
perfon forgotten. In her diet fhe was even
abftemious; and would fometimes pleafantly
boaft, that fhe had fcarce ever tafted wine,
or phyfic; during her whole life. Of the
elegance of drefs fhe had never been fond;
but in her latter life fhe laid it intirely afide;
wearing nothing, for many years, but a clofe
habit of plain, black ferge; which occafioned
many pleafant miftakes between her, and her
attendants.

Her retinue was merely for ufe, not parade.
Befides her common domeftics, fhe had always
two ladies of education, who lived with her.
Many hours fhe fpent alone: at other times,
they read to her, and were her companions.

Her chief expence, as far as concerned herfelf, was in books. Her library was ftored
with all the beft writers in the Englifh language. She knew no other.

Such

Such was the life of this excellent lady; equally fuited to any ftation, in which God had pleafed to place her. It was a life of no more indulgence, than the moft abridged circumftances would have allowed. Her ability in doing good, was that only, in which fhe exceeded others.

She lived twenty-fix years, after the death of her fecond hufband; Providence lengthening out her life, as a bleffing to the country, beyond her eightieth year. The 23d of March 1675 was the day of her diffolution—one of the moft melancholy days the northern counties ever experienced.

In her ended the noble family of the Cliffords. Her daughter Margaret, by the earl of Dorfet (her fole furviving heirefs) marrying the earl of Thanet, carried the Clifford eftates into the Tufton family.*

---

* The moft material part of this little hiftory is taken from a MS. life of Mr. Sedgwick, her fecretary, written by himfelf. In this work Mr. Sedgwick occafionally inferts a few circumftances relating to his lady.—It is a pity he had not given her the better fhare. His MS. is ftill extant in Appelby-caftle.

SECT.

S E C T. XXIV.

FROM Appelby-caftle we foon approach
the barrier-mountains: but we approach
them, in the ufual order of nature, by regular
progrefs. The ground is firft high, before it
becomes mountainous; and tillage appears in
fcanty plots, before cultivation ceafes.

A little to the north of Brugh, the ground
on the left, makes a fingular appearance. A
hill, on which a fair is annually held, forms
an exact, femi-circular convex. Scarce a
knoll, or bufh breaks the regularity of the line.
Beyond this, but without any intervening
ground, rifes a range of diftant mountains.
Thefe wore a light purple hue, when we faw
them—the circular hill, a deep green. Perhaps no difpofition of ground was ever more

totally

totally unpicturefque: and yet even this (fuch
is the force of contraft) if it be only bifected,
and in a fmall degree adorned, is not wholly
difagreeable.

At the commencement of the mountains
ftand the town, and caftle of Brugh, not
unpleafantly feated. The caftle which confifts, like that at Appelby, of two parts,
feems to have been a very ftrong place. Since
the time of it's laft noble inhabitant, the
countefs of Pembroke, it has been falling faft
into ruin; but we found it no eafy matter,
even yet, to fcale the out-works of it's earthen
mounds: fo ftrong a fortrefs hath it once
been.—Some parts of it, efpecially a fhattered
round tower, are very picturefque.

. We had not the opportunity of feeing this
caftle in fo advantageous a light, as had favoured us, when we faw the caftle of Penrith.
We faw them both in the evening; but here
we had no bright beam of fun-fet to *illumine
the ruins*. And yet the effect was grand.
The caftle and landfcape around, were in deep
fhadow; under the influence of a retiring
ftorm, which had hung a fettled gloom on all
                                        the

the upper regions of the fky. The fun was
invifible; but had fired the whole weftern
horizon with a deep red. We viewed the
caftle from the eaft; and had therefore the
ruddy part of the hemifphere as a background
to the grey tints, and ftrong fhadows of the
towers, and battlements, which intervened between us and the weft. Thefe, with the deep
folemnity of the gloom, were a fufficient ba-
lance to the glowing red of the horizon, which
would otherwife have been too glaring. But
the whole was in perfect harmony; and had a
fine effect.—Indeed nature's *colouring* is rarely
without harmony. If the lights be glowing,
the fhades are proportionably deep; on the
contrary, if the lights decay, the fhadows decay with them; and as light is alfo the fource
of colour, the landfcape wears always one uniform hue. Either the *fober colouring* prevails,
or one *vivid tint* fupports another. In *compofition,** we have found, that nature may be improved; but in the beauty, and proportion of
her tints, in the harmony of her *colouring,* fhe
is feldom at variance with herfelf.

---

* See the idea of improving natural compofition, explained,
p. 125, &c. Vol. I.

The

The fquare tower, which made the grand part of the caſtle, conveyed, as we looked into it, a very horrid idea. Moſt of theſe old ſtructures have ſuffered great *external* dilapidations. But here the *ſhell* was intire; and all the *internal* parts were gone—the roof, the ſtories, and even the vault over the dungeon. The whole was a mere excavation. I know not, that I was ever ſtruck with a more horrid idea of the kind. The eye, confined within the walls of a vaſt tower, open to the ſky above, which loured with unuſual blackneſs, looked down with hideous contraſt, deep into a dungeon below.

The whole road, over the mountains of Stainmore, from Brugh-caſtle to Bowes-eaſtle, which is about thirteen miles, is the moſt unpleaſant that can be conceived; and the more ſo, as it reminded us of the ſublime ſcenes, which we had paſſed, in another part of this chain, between Ambleſide and Keſwick. In the mountains of Stainmore, the parts are neither ſufficiently ample to be grand; nor

rich

rich and varied, to be beautiful. We did not
even find what we have elfewhere called *a mere
fcene of mountains.** In fuch a fcene, the *parts*
are beautiful, tho there is no *whole*; but here,
in a picturefque view, there is neither *whole*,
nor *parts*.

Nothing remains of Bowes-caftle, but one
heavy, fquare tower, much defaced, and ruined; tho the ftone-work appears to have been
excellent. This fortrefs feems originally to
have been intended as a defence at the fouthern
end of the mountains; as Brugh-caftle was at
the northern.

From the pofition of thefe caftles, it feems
probable, that formerly the road over the
mountains of Stainmore was the only road into
Cumberland, that was paffable, and of courfe
neceffary to be defended. The Kefwick mountains, till lately, were impervious; and the
mountains of Shap are much fuller of defiles,
and dangerous paffes, than thofe of Stainmore,
which are the moft level, and the moft pene-
trable part of this vaft chain.

---

* See page 168, Vol. I.

As we leave the mountains, a very rich and extensive view opens before us into Yorkshire. We had not seen such a view for many days. For tho in Cumberland, we had many very extensive prospects, yet they extended chiefly over barren country.

At Greta we found much devastation from the late high floods. The bridge was beaten down; and large fragments of it carried away, through the violence of the stream. With these, and huge stones torn from the adjoining cliffs, the bed of the river was choaked. Nothing could have a more ruinous appearance. A *broken bridge* impresses one of the strongest emblems of desolation, from the idea of cutting off all intercourse among men.

Here sir Thomas Robinson has a house,* situated in a pleasant park; one side of which is bounded by the river.

---

* It is now Mr. Morritt's.

The

The road from Greta-bridge leads through a rich country, but open, and unpleasing; unlefs in diftance.

The middle of Gatherly-moor commands a moft extenfive view in every direction. Hambledon-hills bound the profpect in front. On the right ftretches an extent of country towards Richmond. A diftance ftill more remote opens, on the left, into the bifhopric of Durham; and behind rife the mountains of Weftmoreland, as a background to all the wild fcenes we had left.

Few places afford a fituation, where a painter may fee, at once, fo many *modes of diftance*: or where he may better compare, at one glance, their feveral beauties and imperfections.

The wild, unwooded wafte, when thrown into diftance, hath neither variety, nor rich-nefs. It is one uniform, dark, and dreary fpread: unlefs it be happily inlightened; or confift of hilly ground broken into large parts.

The intermixture of tracts of woodland, adds a pleafing variety to diftance; and is adapted to receive the fweeteft effects of light.

But

But the cultivated country forms the moſt amuſing diſtance.* Meadows, corn-fields, hedge-rows, ſpires, towns, and villages, tho loſt as *ſingle objeƈts*, are all melted together into the *richeſt maſs of variegated ſurface*; over which the eye ranges with delight; and following the flitting gleams of ſun-ſhine, catches a thouſand dubious objeƈts, as they ariſe; and creates as many more, which do not really exiſt. But ſuch a country will not bear a nearer approach; eſpecially if it be over-built, which is the caſe of moſt of the rich diſtances about London: the *parts* aſſume too much conſequence, and the *whole* becomes a ſcene of confuſion.

When the death of Elizabeth called James to the crown of England, he took this road from Scotland; and on Gatherly-moor, we are told, he ſtopped to take a view around him; with which he is ſaid to have been greatly delighted. The ſpot, where this royal ſurvey was taken, is ſtill ſhewn—the ſummit of a Roman ſtation.—It is not likely, that

---

* See page 7, Vol. I.

picturefque

picturefque thoughts engaged his princely attention at that time. It is rather probable, that he began there to meafure the length of his new fceptre—for there his wiftful eyes were bleffed with the firft fair profpect of the promifed land.

From Gatherly-moor we entered Leeming-lane; grieved to leave fo much fine country on both fides unfeen. Within a few miles the Tees pouring through a rocky channel, forms fome of the moft romantic fcenery in England; and boafts, at Winfton-bridge, a more magnificent fingle arch, than perhaps any Englifh river can produce.—Within a few miles, in another direction, lie the beautiful, and varied grounds about Richmond; which among other noble fcenes, exhibit the magnificent ruins of a caftle, on the fummit of a lofty rock, over-hanging the Swale.——All this beautiful country we were obliged to leave behind, and enter Leeming-lane, which extends near thirty miles, in a ftraight line, fhut up between hedges; being a part of a great Roman caufey. And yet the whole is fo well planted, that we found it lefs difgufting, than

we

we expected. The fmalleft turn, where the wood hung loofely over the lane, efpecially when there was any variety in the ground, broke the lines, and deftroyed much of the difagreeable regularity of the road.

We left the lane however abruptly, and went to Norton Conyers, near Rippon, the feat of fir Bellingham Graham; from whence we propofed to vifit the neighbouring fcenes of Studley, and Hackfall.

S E C T. XXV.

THE moſt improved part of the gardens at Studley, and what is chiefly ſhewn to ſtrangers, is a valley, nearly circular, ſurrounded by high woody grounds, which ſlope gently into it in various directions. The circumference of the higher grounds includes about one hundred and fifty acres; the area, at the bottom, conſiſts of eight. The higher parts preſent many openings into the country. The lower, of courſe, are more confined; but might afford many pleaſing woody ſcenes, and ſolitary retreats. A conſiderable ſtream runs through the valley: and on the banks of this ſtream, in another valley, contiguous to the circular one, ſtand the ruins of Fountain's abbey; the grandeſt, and moſt beautiful, except perhaps thoſe of Glaſtonbury, which the kingdom can produce.

The

The idea, which fuch vallies naturally fuggeft, is that of retirement—the habitation of chearful folitude. Every object points it out; all tending to footh and amufe: but not to roufe and tranfport; like the great fcenes of nature.

Sometimes indeed the reclufe may be more enamoured of the great fcenes of nature, and wifh to fix his abode, where his eye may be continually prefented with fublime ideas. But in general, we obferve (from the whole hiftory of monaftic life) that he wifhes rather to fequefter himfelf in fome tranquil fcene: and this in particular was chofen as a quiet recefs, confecrated to retirement.

Solitude therefore being the reigning idea of the place, every accompaniment fhould tend to imprefs it. The ruins of the abbey, which is the great object, certainly do. The river and the paths fhould wind carelefly through the lawns and woods, with little decoration. Buildings fhould be fparingly introduced. Thofe which appear, fhould be as fimple as poffible—the mere retreats of folitude. The fcene allows no more; and the neighbourhood of fo noble a ruin renders every
other

other decoration, in the way of building, either trivial, or offenfive.

Inftead of thefe ideas, which the vallies of Studley naturally fuggeft, the whole is a vain oftentation of expence; a mere *Timon's villa*; decorated by a tafte debauched in it's conception, and puerile in it's execution. Not only the reigning idea of the place is forgotten; but all the great mafter-ftrokes of nature, in every fhape, are effaced. Every part is touched and retouched with the infipid fedulity of a Dutch mafter:

———Labor improbus omnia vincit.

What a lovely fcene might a perfon of pure tafte have made at Studley, with one tenth part of the expence, which hath been laid out in deforming it.

Frefh fhadows fit to fhroud from funny ray;
Fair lawns to take the fun in feafon due;
Sweet fprings, in which a thoufand nymphs did play;
Soft, tumbling brooks, that gentle flumber drew;
High reared mounts, the lands about to view;
Low-winding dales, difloigned from common gaze;
Delightful bowers to folace lovers true.

Such might have been the fcenes of Studley: but fuch is the whimfical channel of human

N operations,

operations, that we fometimes fee the pencil of Reubens employed on a country wake; and that of Teniers difgracing the nuptials of an emperor.

On the whole, it is hard to fay, whether nature has done more to embellifh Studley; or art to deform it. Much indeed is below criticifm. But even, where the rules of more genuine tafte have been adopted, they are for the moft part unhappily mifapplied. In the point of opening views, for inftance, few of the openings here are fimple, and natural. The artifice is apparent. The marks of the fheers, and hatchet, are confpicuous in them all. Whereas half the beauty of a thing confifts in the eafinefs of it's introduction. Bring in your ftory awkwardly; and it offends. It is thus in a view. The eye roving at large in queft of objects, cannot bear prefcription. Every thing forced upon it, difgufts; and when it is apparent, that the view is *contrived*; the *effect is loft*.

The valley, in which Fountain's abbey ftands, is not of larger dimenfions, than the other, we have juft defcribed: but inftead of the circular form, it winds (in a more beautiful proportion) into length. It's fides are

compofed

compofed of woody hills floping down in varied
declivities; and uniting with the trees at the
bottom, which adorn the river.

At one end of this valley ftand the ruins of
the abbey, which formerly overfpread a large
fpace of ground. Befides the grand remains
of ruin, there appeared in various parts, among
the trees and bufhes, detached fragments,
which were once the appendages of this great
houfe. One of thefe; which was much admired, feemed evidently to have been a court
of juftice.

Such was the general idea of this beautiful
valley, and of the ruins which adorned it,
before they fell into the hands of the prefent
proprietor. Long had he wifhed to draw them
within the circle of his improvements; but
fome difficulties of law withftood. At length
they were removed; and the time came (which
every lover of picturefque beauty muft lament)
when the legal poffeffion of this beautiful fcene
was yielded to him; and his bufy hands were
let loofe upon it.

A few fragments fcattered around the
body of a ruin are *proper,* and *picturefque.*
They are *proper,* becaufe they account for
what is defaced: and they are *picturefque,*

becaufe

becaufe they unite the principal pile with the
ground; on which union the beauty of compofition, in a good meafure, depends.* But
here they were thought rough and unfightly;
and fell a facrifice to neatnefs. Even the
court of juftice was not fpared; tho a
fragment, probably as beautiful, as it was
curious.

In the room of thefe detached parts,
which were the proper and picturefque em-
bellifhments of the fcene, a gaudy temple is
erected, and other trumpery wholly foreign
to it.

But not only the fcenery is defaced, and the
outworks of the ruin violently torn away; the
main body of the ruin itfelf, is, at this very
time, under the alarming hand of decoration.

The remains of this pile are very magnificent. Almoft the intire fkeleton of the abbey-
church is left, which is a beautiful piece of
Gothic architecture. The tower feems wholly
to have efcaped the injuries of time. It's
mouldering lines only are foftened. Near the
church ftand a double row of cloyfters; which

---

* See the fame idea in mountains, p. 50, Vol. II. and in
building, p. 146, and afterwards in cattle, Sect. XXXI.

are

are fingularly curious from the pointed arches,
which do the office of columns, in fupporting
the roof. At the end of thefe cloyfters ftand
the abbot's apartments; which open into a
court, called the Monk's garden. On one
fide of this court is the hall, a noble room;
which communicates, in the fpirit of hofpi-
tality, with the kitchen. There are befides a
few other detached parts.

When the prefent proprietor made his pur-
chafe, he found this whole mafs of ruin, the
cloyfters, the abbey church, and the hall,
choaked with rubbifh. His firft work therefore was to clear and open. And *fomething*
in this way, might have been done with
propriety. For we fee ruins fometimes fo
choaked, that no view of them can be obtained.

To this bufinefs fucceeded the great work
of *reftoring*, and *ornamenting*. This required
a very delicate touch. Among the ruins were
found fcraps of Gothic windows; fmall, marble columns; tiles of different colours; and a
variety of other ornamental fragments. Thefe
the proprietor has picked from the rubbifh
with great care; and with infinite induftry is
now reftoring to their old fituation. But in

vain;

vain; for the friability of the edges of every fracture makes any restoration of parts an awkward patchwork.

Indeed the very idea of giving a finished splendor to a ruin, is absurd. How unnatural, in a place, evidently forlorn and deserted by man, are the *recent* marks of human industry! —Besides, every sentiment, which the scene suggests, is destroyed. Instead of that soothing melancholy, on which the mind feeds in contemplating the ruins of time; a sort of jargon is excited by these heterogeneous mixtures: as if, when some grand chorus had taken possession of the soul—when the sounds in all their sublimity, were yet vibrating on the ear—a light jig should strike up.

But the *restoration* of parts is not enough; *ornaments* must be added: and such incongruous ornaments, as disgraced the *scene*, are disgracing also the *ruin*. The monk's *garden* is turned into a trim parterre, and planted with flowering shrubs: a view is opened, through the great window, to some ridiculous figure, (I know not what; Ann Bolein, I think, they called it) that is placed in the valley; and in the central part of the abbey-church, a circular pedestal is raised out of the fragments of the
old

old pavement; on which is erected—a muti-
lated heathen ftatue !!!

It is a difficult matter, at the fight of fuch
monftrous abfurdities, to keep refentment
within decent bounds. I hope I have not
exceeded. A *legal* right the proprietor unqueftionably has to deform his ruin, as he
pleafes. But tho he fear no indictment in
the king's bench, he muft expect a very
fevere profecution in the court of tafte. The
refined code of this court does not confider an elegant ruin as a man's *property,*
on which he may exercife at will the
irregular fallies of a wanton imagination:
but as a depofit, of which he is only the
guardian, for the amufement and admiration
of pofterity.—A ruin is a facred thing. Rooted for ages in the foil; affimilated to it; and
become, as it were, a part of it; we confider
it as a work of nature, rather than of art.
Art cannot reach it. A Gothic window, a
fretted arch, fome trivial peculiarity may have
been aimed at with fuccefs: but the *magnificence* of ruin was never attained by any modern
attempt.

What

What reverence then is due to thefe facred relics ; which the rough hand of temerity, and caprice dare mangle without remorfe? The leaft error is irretrievable. Let us paufe a moment.——A Goth may deform : but it exceeds the power of art to amend.

The fcenes of Studley, which I have here defcribed, are confined to the two contiguous vallies. The improvements of the place extend confiderably farther : but we had neither time, nor inclination, to examine more. We had feen enough.

About the clofe of the laft century, a piece of human antiquity exifted in the neighbourhood of this abbey, ftill more curious, than the abbey itfelf—that venerable inftance of longevity, Henry Jenkins. Among all the events, which, in the courfe of a hundred and fixty-nine years, had faftened upon the memory of this fingular man, he fpoke of nothing with fo much emotion, as the ancient ftate of Fountain's abbey. If he were ever queftioned on that fubject, he would be fure to inform you,

" What

"What a brave place it had once been;" and would fpeak with much feeling of the clamour, which it's diffolution occafioned in the coun-try.* "About a hundred and thirty years ago, he would fay, when I was butler to lord Conyers, and old Marmaduke Bradley, now dead and gone, was lord abbot, I was often fent by my lord to inquire after the lord-abbot's health; and the lord abbot would always fend for me up into his chamber, and would order me roaft-beef;† and waffel; which I remember well, was always brought in a *black-jack.*"——From this account we fee what it was that rivetted Fountain's abbey fo diftinctly in the old man's memory. The *black-jack*, I doubt not, was a ftronger idea, than the fplendor of the houfe, or the virtues of the lord-abbot.

---

* The *fubftance* of thefe particulars the author had from a MS. fhewn him by fir Bellingham Graham.

† The MS. fays, *a quarter of a yard* of roaft-beef. I have heard that the monafteries ufed to meafure out their beef; but in what way I never underftood.

SECT.

S E C T.   XXVI.

FROM Studley we vifited the fcenes of Hackfall. Thefe own the fame proprietor; and are adorned with equal tafte.

It is a circumftance of great advantage, to be carried to this grand exhibition (as you always fhould be) through the *clofe lanes* of the Rippon road. You have not the leaft intimation of a defign upon you; nor any fuggeftion, that you are on high grounds; till the folding-doors of the building at Mowbray-point being thrown open, you are ftruck with one of the grandeft, and moft beautiful burfts of country, that the imagination can form.

Your eye is firft carried many fathoms precipitately down a bold, woody fteep, to the river Ewer, which forms a large femi-circular

curve

curve below; winding to the very foot of the precipice, on which you ſtand. The trees of the precipice over-hang the central part of the curve.

In other parts too the river is intercepted by woods; but enough of it is diſcovered to leave the eye at no uncertainty in tracing it's courſe. At the two oppoſite points of the curve, two promontories ſhoot into the river, in contraſt with each other: that on the right is woody, faced with rock, and crowned with a caſtle: that, on the left, riſes ſmooth from the water, and is ſcattered over with a few clumps. The peninſular part, and the grounds alſo at ſome diſtance beyond the iſthmus, conſiſt of one intire woody tract; which advancing boldly to the foot of the precipice, unites itſelf with it.

This woody ſcenery on the banks of the river may be called the firſt diſtance. Beyond this lies a rich, extenſive country—broken into large parts—decorated with all the objects, and diverſified with all the tints of diſtant landſcape—retiring from the eye, ſcene after ſcene—till at length every vivid hue fading gradually away, and all diſtinction of parts being loſt, the country imperceptibly

melts

melts into the horizon; except where the blue hills of Hambledon clofe the view.

Through the whole extent of this grand fcene—this delightful gradation of light and colours—nature has wrought with her broadeft, and freeft pencil. The parts are ample: the compofition perfectly correct. She hath admitted nothing difgufting, or even trivial. I fcarce remember any where an extenfive view fo full of beauties, and, at the fame time, fo free from faults. Nothing difgufts. The foreground is as pleafing as the background; which it never can be, when plots of cultivation approach the eye: and it is rare to find fo large an extent of near-ground, covered by wood, or other furface, whofe parts are alike grand, and beautiful.

The vale, of which this view is compofed, hath not yet intirely loft it's ancient name— the *vale of Mowbray*; fo called from Mowbray-caftle now no longer traced even in it's ruins; but once fuppofed to be the capital manfion of thefe wide domains. This vale extends from York almoft to the confines of Durham; is adorned by the Swale, and the Ewer, both confiderable rivers; and is certainly

tainly one of the nobleſt tracts of country
of the kind in England.

Hackfall is as much a contraſt to Studley,
as the idea of *magnificence* is to that of *ſolitude*.
It requires of courſe a different mode of ornament. A banqueting houſe, inriched with
every elegance of architecture, in the form
perhaps of a Grecian temple, might' be a
proper decoration at Mowbray-point; which
at Studley would be ſuperfluous, and abſurd.
The ruins of a caſtle too, if they *could* be executed with veri-ſimilitude and grandeur, might
adorn the rocky promontory on the right with
propriety. The preſent ruin is a paltry thing.
Any other ornamental building, beſides theſe
two, I ſhould ſuppoſe unneceſſary. Theſe
might ſufficiently adorn every part of the
ſcenery, both in the higher, and in the lower
grounds. If the expence, which is generally
laid out, in our great gardens, on a variety
of *little* buildings, was confined to one or
two *capital objects*, the general effect would
be better. A profuſion of buildings is one
of the extravagances of falſe taſte. *One* object is a proper ornament in every ſcene: more
than

than one, at leaſt on the foregrounds, diſtract it. Particular circumſtances indeed may add a *propriety* to a greater number of objects: as at Kew; where a ſpecimen is given of different kinds of religious ſtructures: or at Chiſwick; where it is intended to exhibit an idea of various modes of architecture. But it is *unity* of *deſign*, not of *picmreſque compoſition*, which pleaſes in theſe ſcenes. As far as this is concerned, one handſome object is enough.

Having examined the whole of this very extraordinary burſt of landſcape from Mowbray-point, we deſcended to the bottom, where a great variety of grand, and pleaſing views are exhibited; particularly a view of Mowbray-point from Limus-hill; and another of the promontory with the caſtle upon it, from the tent: and it muſt be acknowledged, that many of theſe views are opened in a very natural, and maſterly manner. If any art hath been uſed, it hath been uſed with diſcretion.

At the ſame time, amidſt all this profuſion of great objects, and all this grandeur of *de-*

ſign

fign (for nature has here not only brought her materials together, but has compofed them likewife) the eye is every where called afide from the contemplation of them by fome trivial object—an awkward cafcade—a fountain— a view through a hole cut in a wood—or fome other ridiculous fpecimen of abfurd tafte.

It is a great happinefs however, that the improver of thefe fcenes had lefs in his power at Hackfall, than he had at Studley. The vallies there, and home-views were all within the reach of his fpade, and axe. Here he could only contemplate at a diftance what glorious fcenes he might have difplayed, if his arm could have extended to the horizon. Some of the nearer grounds of this grand exhibition, (I believe all beyond the Ewer,) are the property of another perfon. So that the whole peninfular part, and the grounds immediately beyond it, continue facred, and untouched : and thefe are the fcenes, which form the grand part of the view from Mowbray-point. In furveying thefe, the eye overlooks the *puerilities of improvement* at the bottom of the precipice.

The

The banks of rivers are fo various, that I know not any two river-views of any celebrity, which at all refemble each other in the *detail*; tho in the *general caft*, and *outlines* of the fcene, they may agree. Thus at Studley, and at * Corby, the materials of the fcenery are, in both places, the fame. Each hath it's woody banks—it's river—and the ruins of an abbey. In each alfo the beauties of the fcene are in a great meafure fhut up in a valley within itfelf; and the idea of folitude is impreffed on both. Notwithftanding this fimilarity, two fcenes can hardly be more different. At Corby, the woody bank is grander than that at Studley, bordering rather on the fublime. At Studley, the form and contraft of the vallies, and the great variety of the ground, is more pleafing. In the former fcene the river is fuperior: in the latter, the ruins. In one, you wander about the mazes of a circular woody bank : in the other, the principal part of the walk is con- tinued along the margin of the river; the

---

* See page 102.

woody bank, which is too fteep to admit a path, ferving only as a fkreen.

There is the fame union and difference between the fcenes of Persfield,* and Hackfall. Both are *great* and *commanding* fituations. The river, in both, forms a *fweeping curve.* Both are adorned with *rocks, and woods:* and fublimity is the reigning idea of each. Notwithftanding all thefe points of union, they are wholly unlike. Persfield, tho the country is open before it, depends little on it's beauties. It's own wild, winding banks fupply an endlefs variety of rocky fcenery; which is fufficient to engage the attention. The banks of Hackfall are lefs magnificent; tho it's river is more picturefque, and it's woods more beautiful. But it's views into the country are it's pride; and beyond any comparifon, grander and more inchanting, than thofe at Persfield.

From Hackfall we returned to our hofpitable quarters at *Norton Conyers,* which is

---

* See obfervations on the Wye, page 39.

fituated

fituated in a pleafant park-fcene; but too flat
to admit much variety.

In the time of the civil wars, the owner of
this manfion was Sir Richard Graham; of
whom we heard an anecdote in the family,
which is worth relating; as it is not only
curious in itfelf, but throws a very ftrong,
and yet natural fhade, on the character of
Cromwell.

When the affairs of Charles I. were in
their wane in all the fouthern counties; the
marquifs of Newcaftle's prudence gave them
fome credit in the north. His refidence was
at York, where he engaged two of the gentlemen of the country to act under him as
lieutenants. Sir Richard Graham was one;
whofe commiffion under the marquifs is ftill
in the hands of the family. As Sir Richard
was both an active man, and much attached
to the royal caufe; he entered into it with
all that vigour, which ability, infpired by inclination, could exert; and did the king more
effectual fervice, than perhaps any private
gentleman in thofe parts.

On that fatal day, when the precipitancy
of prince Rupert, in oppofition to the fage

advice

advice of the marquifs, led the king's forces out of York againft Cromwell, who waited for them on Marfden-moor, Sir Richard Graham had a principal command; and no man did more than he, to end an action with fuc-cefs, which had been undertaken with teme-rity.

When the day was irretrievably loft; and nothing remained, but for every man to feek the beft means of fecurity that offered, Sir Richard fled, with twenty-fix bleeding wounds upon him, to his own houfe at Norton Con-yers, about fifteen miles from the field. Here he arrived in the evening: and being fpent with lofs of blood, and fatigue, he was car-ried into his chamber; where taking a laft farewell of his difconfolate lady, he expired.

Cromwell, who had ever expreffed a pecu-liar inveteracy againft this gentleman, and thought a victory only half obtained, if he efcaped; purfued his flight in perfon, with a troop of horfe.

When he arrived at Norton, his gallant enemy was dead; having fcarce lived an hour, after he was carried into his chamber: and Cromwell found his wretched lady weeping over

over the mangled corpfe of her hufband, yet fcarce cold.

Such a fight, one fhould have imagined, might have given him—not indeed an emotion of pity—but at leaft a fatiety of revenge. The inhuman mifcreant ftill felt the vengeance of his foul unfatisfied; and turning round to his troopers, who had ftalked after him into the facred receffes of forrow, he gave the fign of havoc; and in a few moments the whole houfe was torn to pieces: not even the bed was fpared, on which the mangled body was extended: and every thing was deftroyed, which the hands of rapine could not carry off.

In this country we met with another curious memorial of the battle of Marfden-moor. A carpenter, about two years ago, bought fome trees, which had grown there. But when the timber was brought to the faw-pit, it was found very refractory. On examining it with more attention, it appeared, that great numbers of leaden bullets were in the hearts of feveral of the trees; which thus recorded the very fpot, where the heat of the battle had raged.

SECT.

(...)

S E C T. XXVII.

FROM Norton we propofed to take our
rout, through Yorkfhire into Derbyfhire; and fo through the other midland
counties into the fouth of England.

The town of Rippon makes a better appearance, as you approach it, than the generality of country towns. The church is a
large building; and gives a confequence to
the place.

From Rippon the road is not unpleafant;
paffing generally through a woody country,
till we entered Knarefborough-foreft, where
all wood ceafed. Like other royal chafes, it
hath now loft all it's fylvan honours, and is
a wild, bleak, unornamented tract of country.

Near

Near the clofe of the foreft, lies Harrogate, in the dip of a hill; a cheerlefs, unpleafant village. Nor does the country make any change for the better; till we crofs the river Wharf.

From hence, leaving the ruins of Harewood-caftle on the left, and Harewood-houfe on the right, we afcended, by degrees, a tract of high ground, and had an extenfive view which was illumined, when we faw it, by thofe gleaming, curfory lights, which are fo beautiful in diftant landfcape; and fo common, when the incident of a bright fun, a windy fky, and floating clouds coincide. It is amufing, under thefe circumftances, to purfue the flitting gleams, as they fpread, decay, and vanifh—then rife in fome other part; varied by the different furfaces, over which they fpread.

We have this appearance beautifully detailed in an old Erfe poem, the title of which is Dargo. The bard poetically, and picturefquely

refquely compares the fhort tranfitions of joy
in the mind, to thefe tranfitory gleams of
light.

" The tales of the years that are paft, are
beams of light to the foul of the bard. They
are like the fun-beams, that travel over the
heaths of Morven. Joy is in their courfe,
tho darknefs dwells around. Joy is in their
courfe; but it is foon paft: the fhades of
darknefs purfue them: they overtake them
on the mountains; and the footfteps of the
cheerful beam are no longer difcovered.—Thus
the tale of Dargo travels over my foul like
a beam of light, tho the gathering of the
clouds is behind."

We fhould have been glad to have examined Harewood-houfe, as it is a fumptuous
pile; but it is fhewn only on particularly days;
and we happened to be there on a wrong one.

We regretted alfo another misfortune of
the fame kind, for which we had only ourfelves to blame; and that was the omiffion
of Kirkftall-abbey. In the precipitancy of
an

an early morning, and through an unaccountable error in geography, we paſſed it; and
did not recollect the miſtake, till we were
half a day's journey beyond it.

Around Leeds the ſoil wears an unpleaſant
hue; owing in part to the dirtineſs of the
ſurface; within a few yards of which, coal
is every where found.—The country however
changes greatly for the better, before we arrive at Wakefield, which lie in the midſt
of beautiful ſcenery. The river Calder makes
a fine appearance, as we leave the town;
and it's banks are adorned by a Gothic chapel, now in ruins, dedicated by Edward IV,
to the memory of the duke of York, his father, and the other chiefs of his party, who
fell at the battle of Wakefield. It is built
in the elegant proportion of ten by ſix; plain
on the ſides; but richly adorned on the front;
and finiſhed with a ſmall octagon turret at
the eaſt end.—This little edifice ſerves both
to aſcertain the hiſtory of architecture, which
appears to have been near it's meridian; and
to illuſtrate an important part of the Engliſh
ſtory. It's whimſical ſituation by the ſide
of

of a bridge, was intended probably to mark
the spot, where some principal part of the
action happened: tho at the entrance of great
towns it was not unusual, in popish times,
to place chapels on bridges; that travellers
might immediately have the benefit of a mass:
There was, for this purpose, a chapel formerly
in one of the piers of London-bridge.

Not far from Wakefield we rode past a
piece of water, which takes the humble name
of a mill-pond; but is in fact a beautiful
little lake; being near two miles in circumference, and containing some pleasing scenery,
along it's little woody shores, and promontories.

From Bank-top we had a good descending
view of Wentworth-castle—of the grounds,
which inviron it—and the country, which
surrounds it. The whole together is grand.
The eminence, on which we stood, is adorned
with a great profusion of something, in the
way of an artificial ruin. It is possible it
may have an effect from the castle below:
but

but *on the spot*, it is certainly no ornament. We found some difficulty in passing through lord Strafford's park; and proceeded therefore to Wentworth-house; which is a superb; and is esteemed, an elegant pile: but there seems to be a great want of simplicity about it. The front appears broken into too many parts; and the inside, incumbered. A simple plan has certainly more dignity. Such, for instance, is lord Tilney's house at Wanstead, where the whole is intelligible *at sight*. The hall at lord Rockingham's is a cube of sixty feet. The gallery is what they call a *shelf*. For myself, I saw nothing offensive in it, tho it is undoubtedly a more masterly contrivance to raise a gallery *upon* a wall, than to affix one *to it*. The long gallery is a noble apartment; and the interception of a breakfast room from it by pillars, and an occasional curtain, gives a pleasant combined idea of retirement, and company. The library also is grand.

There are few good good pictures at Wentworth. The original of lord Strafford, and his secretary, is said to be here. It's pretensions are disputed; tho I think it has merit enough to maintain them any where.——There is
another

another good portrait by Vandyke of the fame nobleman. He refts his hand upon a dog; and his head in this picture is perhaps fuperior to that of the other.—Here is alfo, by Vandyke, a fon of the fame earl, with his two fifters. The management of the whole difpleafes; but the boy is delightfully painted.

Wentworth-houfe ftands low. It's front commands an extenfive plain, and a flat diftant country; which are feen betwixt a rifing wood on the left; and a variety of croffing lawns on the right. On the whole, we were not much pleafed with any thing we faw here.

SECT. XXVIII.

FROM Wentworth-houfe the fame pleafant face of country continues to Sheffield.
But it foon begins to change, as we approach
Derbyfhire. The rifing grounds become in-
fenfibly more wild: rocks ftart every where
from the foil; and a new country comes on
apace. For we now approached that great
central tract of high lands; which arifing
in thefe parts, form themfelves into mountains; and fpreading here, and there, run on
without interruption, as far as Scotland.*
Before we reach Middleton, the whole face
of the land has fuffered change; and we fee
nothing around us, but wildnefs and defola-
tion.

---

* See page 3, Vol. I.

About

About two miles fhort of Middleton we are cheared again by a beautiful valley; which participates indeed of the wildnefs of the country; but is both finely wooded, and watered. In a recefs of this valley ftands Middleton, a very romantic village; beyond which the valley ftill continues two miles farther.

It is this *continuation* of it, which is known by the name of Middleton-dale; and is efteemed one of the moft romantic fcenes of the country. It is a narrow, winding chafm; hardly broader than to give fpace for a road. On the right, it is rocky; on the left, the hills wear a fmoother form. The rocks are grey, tinged in many parts with plots of ver-dure infinuating themfelves, and running among them. Some of thefe rocks affume a peculiar form, rearing themfelves like the round towers, and buttreffes of a ruined caftle; and their upper ftrata running in parallel directions, take the form of cornices. The *turriti fcopuli* of Virgil cannot be illuftrated better. I fhould not however affirm, they are the more pic-turefque on this account. Nature's ufual forms, when beautiful in their kind, are gene-rally the moft beautiful.

When

When we leave Middleton-dale the waftes of Derbyfhire open before us; and wear the fame face as thofe we had left behind, on the borders of Yorkfhire. They are tracts of coarfe, moorifh pafturage, forming vaft con-vex fweeps, without any interfection of line, or variation of ground; divided into portions by ftone walls, without a cottage to diverfify the fcene, or a tree to enliven it. Middleton-dale is the pafs, which unites thefe two dreary fcenes.

Having travelled feveral miles in this high country, in our way to Caftleton, we came at length to the edge of a precipice; down which ran a long, fteep defcent. From the brow, an extenfive vale lay before us. It's name is Hope-dale. It is a wide, open fcene of cultivation; the fides of which, tho moun-tainous, are tilled to the top. The village of Hope ftands at one end of it, and Caftleton at the other. In a direction towards the middle of this vale we defcended. The object of our purfuit, was that celebrated chafm, near Caftleton, called the *Devil's cave*.

P A defcent

A defcent of two miles brought us to it.—
A combination of more horrid ideas is rarely
found, than this place affords. It exceeded
our livelieft imagination.

A rocky mountain rifes to a great height:
in moft parts perpendicular; in fome, beetling
over it's bafe. As it afcends, it divides;
forming at the top, two rocky fummits.—
On one of thefe fummits ftands an old caftle;
the battlements of which appear to grow out
of the rock. It's fituation, on the edge of a
precipice, is tremendous. Looking up from
the bottom, you may trace a narrow path,
formed merely by the adventrous foot of curiofity, winding here and there round the walls
of the caftle; which, as far as appears, is the
only road to it.—The other rock referves it's
terrors for the bottom. There it opens into
that tremendous chafm, called the Devil's
cave. Few places have more the air of the
poetical regions of Tartarus.

The combination of a caftle, and a cave,
which we have here in *reality*, Virgil *feigns*—
with a view perhaps of giving an additional
terror to each.

Æneas

———Ænéas arces, quibus altus Apollo
Præfidet, horrendæque procul fecreta Sibyllæ,
Antrum immane, petit———

The poet does not give the detail of his *antrum
immane*: if he had, he could not have conceived more interefting circumftances, than are
here brought together.

A towering rock hangs over you; under
which you enter an arched cavern, twelve yards
high, forty wide, and near a hundred long.
So vaft a canopy of *unpillared* rock ftretching
over your head, gives you an involuntary fhud-
der. A ftrong light at the mouth of the cave,
difplays all the horrors of the *entrance* in full
proportion. But this light decaying, as you
proceed, the imagination is left to explore it's
deeper caverns by torch-light, which gives
them additional terror. At the end of the firft
cavern runs a river, about forty feet wide,
over which you are ferried into a fecond, of
dimenfions vafter than the firft. It is known
by the name of the Cathedral. The height of
it is horribly difcovered by a few fpiracles at
the top; through which you fee the light of
the day, without being able, at fuch a diftance,
to enjoy the leaft benefit from it. It may
be called a kind of ftar-light. Beyond this

P 2   cavern

cavern flows another branch of the fame river, which becomes the boundary of other caverns ftill more remote. But this was farther than we chofe to proceed. I never found any picturefque beauty in the interior regions of the earth; and the idea growing too infernal, we were glad to return

————cœli melioris ad aurás.

The inhabitants of thefe fcenes are as favage as the fcenes themfelves. We were reminded by a difagreeable contraft of the pleafing fimplicity and civility of manners, which we found among the lakes and mountains of Cumberland. Here a wild, uninformed ftare, through matted, difhevelled locks, marks every feature; and the traveller is followed, like a fpectacle, by a croud of gazers. Many of thefe miferable people live under the tremendous roof we have juft defcribed; where a manufacture of ropeyarn is carried on. One poor wretch has erected a hut within it's verge, where fhe has lived thefe forty years. A little ftraw fuffices for a roof, which has only to refift the droppings of unwholefome vapour from the top of the cavern.

The

The exit from Hope-dale, in our road to
Buxton, is not inferior to the fcene we had
left. We afcend a ftraining fteep, ornamented
on each fide, with bold projecting rocks,
moft of which are picturefque; tho fome of
them are rather fantaftic.

. As we leave this pafs, on our right appears
Mam-tor, furnamed the *Shivering mountain*.
A part of it's fide has the appearance of a cafcade; down which it continually difcharges
the flaky fubftance, of which it is compofed.

On the confines of this mountain, and but
a little below the furface, is found that curious,
variegated mineral, which is formed into fmall
ornamental obelifks, urns and vafes. It is
fuppofed to be a petrifaction; and is known in
London by the name of the *Derbyfhire drop*.
But on the fpot it is called *Blue John*, from
the blue veins, which overfpread the fineft
parts of it. Where it wears a yellowifh hue,
the vein is coarfeft: in many parts it is beau-

tifully

tifully honeycombed, and tranſparent. The proprietors of the marble works at Aſhford farmed the quarry of this curious mineral, laſt year, at ninety-five pounds ; and it is thought have nearly exhauſted it.

From Hope-dale to Buxton, the country is dreary, and uncomfortable. The eye ranges over bleak waſtes, ſuch as we had ſeen before, divided every where by ſtone walls. The paſturage in many parts ſeems good, as the fields were ſtocked with cattle ; but hardly a tree, or a houſe appears through the whole diſtrict.

In a bottom, in this uncomfortable country, lies Buxton, ſurrounded with dreary, barren hills ; and ſteaming, on every ſide, with offenſive lime kilns. Nothing, but abſolute want of health, could make a man endure a ſcene ſo wholly diſguſting.

Near Buxton we viſited another horrid cave, called *Pool's hole* ; but it wants thoſe magnificent accompaniments of *external* ſcenery, which we found at the Devil's cave.

The

The fame dreary face of country continues from Buxton to Aſhford. Here we fall into a beautiful vale fringed with wood, and watered by a brilliant ſtream, which recalled to our memory the pleaſing ſcenes of this kind we had met with among the mountains of Cumberland.

At Aſhford is carried on a manufactory of marble dug on the ſpot; ſome of which, curiouſly incruſted with ſhells, is very beautiful.

The vale of Aſhford continues with little interruption to Bakewell, where it enters another ſweet vale—the vale of Haddon; ſo ealled from Haddon-hall, a magnificent old manſion, which ſtands in the middle of it, on a rocky knoll, incompaſſed with wood.

This princely ſtructure, ſcarce yet in a ſtate of ruin, is able, it is ſaid, to trace it's origin into times before the conqueſt. It then wore a military form. In after ages, it became

P 4   poſſeſſed

poffeffed by different noble families; and about the beginning of this century was inhabited by the dukes of Rutland. Since that time, it has been neglected. Many fragments of it's ancient grandeur remain—fculptured chimnies; fretted cornices; patches of coftly tapeftry;

Aurataſque trabes, veterum decora alta parentum.

Not far from hence lies Chatfworth, in a fituation naturally bleak; but rendered not unpleafant by the accompaniments of well-grown wood.

Chatfworth was the glory of the laft age, when trim parterres, and formal water-works were in fafhion. It *then* acquired a celebrity, which it has never loft; tho it has *now* many rivals. A good approach has been made to it; but in other refpects, when we faw it, it's invirons had not kept pace with the improvements of the times. Many of the old formalities remained. But a dozen years, no doubt, have introduced much improvement.

The houfe itfelf would have been no way ftriking; except in the wilds of Derbyfhire. The chapel is magnificent. It is adorned, on

the

the whole of one fide, by a painting in frefco, reprefenting Chrift employed in works of charity.

There are few pictures in the houfe. A portrait of the late duke of Cumberland by Reynolds was the beft. But there is much exquifite carving by the hand of Gibbons. We admired chiefly the dead fowl of various kinds, with which the chimney of one of the ftate rooms is adorned. It is aftonifhing to fee the downy foftnefs of feathers given to wood. The particulars however alone are admirable: Gibbons was no adept at compofition.

From Chatfworth, through Darley-dale, a fweet, extenfive fcene, we approached Matlock.

The rocky fcenery about the bridge is the firft grand fpecimen of what we were to expect.

As we advanced towards the boat-houfe, the views became more interefting.

Soon after the *great Torr* appeared, which is a moft magnificent rock, decorated with wood and ftained with various hues, yellow, green, and grey.—On the oppofite fide, the rocks, contracting the road, flope diagonally.

Thefe ftraits open into the vale of Matlock; a romantic, and moft delightful fcene, in which
the

the ideas of fublimity and beauty are blended
in a high degree. It extends about two miles
in length; and in the wideft parts is half a
mile broad. The area confifts of much irregular ground. The right hand bank has little
confequence, except that of fhaping the vale.
It is the left hand bank which ennobles the
fcene. This very magnificent rampart, rifing
in a femi-circular form, is divided into four
ample faces of rock, with an interruption of
wood between each. The firft, which you
approach, is the higheft; but of leaft extent:
the next fpreads more; and the third moft of all.
A larger interruption fucceeds; and the laft,
in comparifon of the others, feems but a gentle
effort. The whole rampart is beautifully
fhaded with wood; which in fome places,
grows among the cliffs, garnifhing the rocks—
in others, it grows wildly among thofe breaks,
and interruptions, which feparate their feveral
faces. The *fummit* of the whole femi-circular
range is finely adorned with fcattered trees,
which often break the hard lines of the rock;
and by admitting the light, give an airinefs to
the whole.

The

The river Derwent, which winds under this
femi-circular fcreen, is a broken, rapid ftream.
In fome places only, it is vifible: in others,
delving among rocks, and woody projections,
it is an object only to the ear.

It is impoffible to view fuch fcenes as thefe,
without feeling the imagination take fire.
Little fairy fcenes, where the parts, tho trifling,
are happily difpofed; fuch, for inftance, as the
cafcade-fcene * in the gardens at the Leafowes,
pleafe the fancy. But this is fcenery of a different kind. Every object here, is fublime,
and wonderful. Not only the eye is pleafed;
but the imagination is filled. We are carried
at once into the fields of fiction, and romance.
Enthufiaftic ideas take poffeffion of us; and we
fuppofe ourfelves among the inhabitants of fa-
bled times.—The tranfition indeed is eafy and
natural, from romantic fcenes to romantic
inhabitants.

————————————Sylvis fcena corufcis
Defuper, horrentique atrum nemus imminet umbra;
Nympharum domus————

* See page 59, Vol. I.

The

The woods here are subject to one great inconvenience——that of periodical lopping. About seven years ago, I had the mortification to see almost the whole of this scenery displaying one continued bald face of rock. It is now,* I should suppose, in perfection. More wood would cover, and less would dismantle it†.

The *exit* of this bold romantic scene, (which from the south is the *entrance* into it,) like the exit from Hope-dale, is equal to the scene itself. Grand rocks arise on each side, and dismiss you through a winding barrier, which lengthens out the impression of the scene, like the vibration of a sound. In some parts the solid stone is cut through;

Admittitque viam sectæ per viscera rupis,

---

* In the year 1772.

† This whole side of the river is now, I am told, in the hands of a proprietor, who will not allow the wood to be lopped periodically any more. It may however be suffered to become too luxuriant; and efface the rock.

From

From hence to Afhburn the road is pleafant, after the firft fteeps. The ground is varied, and adorned with wood; and we lofe all thofe wild fcenes, which we met with in the Peak. When nature throws her *wild fcenes* into beautiful compofition; and decorates them with great, and noble objects; they are, of all others, the moft engaging. But as there is little of this decoration in the *wild fcenes of the Peak*, we left them without regret.

S E C T. XXIX.

FROM Afhburn, which is among the larger villages, and ftands fweetly, we made an excurfion to *Dove-dale*.

Dove-dale is the continuation of another fimilar dale, which is fometimes called *Bunfter-dale*; tho I believe both parts of the valley are known, except juft on the fpot, by the general name of Dove-dale.

Bunfter-dale opens with a grand craggy mountain on the right. As you look up to the cliffs, which form the irregular fides of this precipice, your guide will not fail to tell you the melancholy fate of a late dignitary of the church, who riding along the top of it with a young lady, behind him, and purfuing a track, which happened to be

only

only a sheep-path, and led to a declivity; fell in attempting to turn his horse out of it. He was killed; but the young lady was caught by a bush, and saved.—A dreadful story is an admirable introduction to an awful scene. It rouses the mind; and adds double terror to every precipice.

The bare sides of these lofty craggs on the right, are contrasted by a woody mountain on the left. In the midst of the wood, a sort of rocky-wall rises perpendicular from the soil. These detached rocks are what chiefly characterize the place.—A little beyond them, we enter, what is properly called, Dove-dale.

From the description given of Dove-dale, even by men of taste, we had conceived it to be a scene rather of curiosity, than of beauty. We supposed the rocks were formed into the most fantastic shapes; and expected to see a gigantic display of all the conic sections. But we were agreeably deceived. The whole composition is chaste, and picturesquely beautiful, in a high degree.

On

On the right, you have a continuation of the fame grand, craggy mountain, which ran along Bunfter-dale; only the mountain in Dove-dale is higher, and the rocks ftill more majeftic, and more detached.

On the left, is a continuation alfo of the fame hanging woods, which began in Bunfter-dale. In the midft of this woody fcenery arifes a grand, folitary, pointed rock, the charateriftic feature of the vale; which by way of eminence is known by the name of Dove-dale-church. It confifts of a large face of rock, with two or three little fpiry heads, and one very large one: and tho the form is rather peculiar, yet it is pleafing. It's rifing a fingle objet among furrounding woods takes away the fantaftic idea; and gives it fublimity. It is the multiplicity of thefe fpiry heads, which makes them difgufting: as when we fee feveral of them adorning the fummits of alpine mountains*. But a *folitary* rock, tho fpiry, has often a' good effet. A picturefque ornament of this kind, marks a beautiful fcene, at a place

---

* See page 81, Vol. I.

Q called

called the *New-Weir*, on the banks of the Wye.*

The colour of all thefe rocks is *grey*; and harmonizes agreeably with the verdure, which runs in large patches down their channelled fides. Among all the picturefque accompaniments of rocks, nothing has a finer effect in painting, than this variation and contraft of colour, between the cold, grey hue of a rocky furface, and the rich tints of herbage.

The valley of Dove-dale is very narrow at the bottom, confifting of little more than the channel of the Dove, which is a confiderable ftream; and of a foot-path along it's banks. When the river rifes, it fwells over the whole area of the valley; and has a fine effect. The grandeur of the river is then in full harmony with the grandeur of it's banks.

Dove-dale is a calm, fequeftered fcene; and yet not wholly the haunt of folitude, and contemplation. It is too magnificent, and too interefting a piece of landfcape, to leave the mind wholly difengaged.

---

* See obfervations on the Wye, page 24.

The

The late Dr. Brown, comparing the fcenery here, with that of Kefwick,* tells us,
that *of the three circumftances, beauty, horror,
and immenfity* (by which laft he means *grandeur)* of which Kefwick confifts, the fecond
alone is found in Dove-dale.

In this defcription he feems, in my opinion,
juft to have inverted the truth. It is difficult
to conceive, why he fhould either rob Dove-
dale of *beauty,* and *grandeur;* or fill it with
horror. If *beauty* confift in a pleafing arrange-
ment of pleafing parts, Dove-dale has certainly a great fhare of *beauty.* If *grandeur*
confift in large parts, and large objects, it
has certainly *grandeur* alfo. But if *horror*
confift in the vaftnefs of thofe parts, it certainly predominates lefs here, than in the regions of Kefwick. The hills, the woods,
and the rocks of Dove-dale are fufficient to
raife the idea of *grandeur;* but not to imprefs
that of *horror.*

On the whole, Dove-dale is perhaps one
of the moft pleafing pieces of fcenery of the
kind we any where meet with. It has fome-

* In a letter to lord Lyttelton, already quoted.

Q 2   thing

thing in it peculiarly charaĉteriſtic. It's detached, perpendicular rocks ſtamp it with
an image intirely it's own: and for that rea-
ſon it affords the greater pleaſure. For it
is in landſcape, as in life; we are moſt ſtruck
with the peculiarity of an original charaĉter;
provided there is nothing offenſive in it.

From Dove-dale we proceeded to Ilam;
which is another very charaĉteriſtic ſcene.

Ilam ſtands on a hill, which ſlopes gently
in front; but is abrupt, and broken behind,
where it is garniſhed with rock, and hanging
wood. Round this hill ſweeps a ſemi-cir-
cular valley; the area of which is a flat meadow, nearly a quarter of a mile in breadth,
and twice as much in circumference. At the
extremity of the meadow winds the channel
of a river, confiderable in it's dimenſions;
tho penurioufly ſupplied with water: and beyond all, ſweeps a grand, woody bank, which
forms a background to the ſcenery behind the
houfe; and yet, in the front, admits a view
of diftant mountains; particularly of that
ſquare-capt hill, called Thorp-cloud, which
ſtands near the entrance of Dove-dale.

Befides

Befides the *beauty* of the place, we are prefented with a great *curiofity*. The river *Manifold* formerly ran in that channel under the woody bank, which we obferved to be now fo penurioufly fupplied.—It has deferted it's ancient bed; and about feven miles from Ilam, enters gradually the body of a mountain; under which it forces a way, and continues it's fubterraneous rout as far as the hill, on which Ilam ftands. There it rifes from the ground, and forms a river in a burft. The channel under the bank is a fort of wafte-pipe to it; carrying off the fuperfluity of water, which in heavy rains cannot enter the mountain.

Curious this river certainly is: but were it mine, I fhould wifh much to check it's fubterraneous progrefs, and throw it into it's old channel. The ouzy bed, which is now a deformity, would then be an object of beauty, circling the meadow with a noble ftream.—Another deformity alfo would be avoided, that of cutting the meadow with two channels.—Or perhaps all ends might be anfwered, if the wafte-ftream could be diverted. Then both the curiofity; and, in a good degree, the beauty, would remain.

On

On the whole, we have few fituations fo pleafingly romantic, as Ilam. The rocky hill it ftands on; the ample lawn, which incircles it; the bold, woody bank, which invirons the whole (where pleafing walks might be formed) the bold incurfion of the river; the views into the country; and the neighbourhood of Dove-dale, which lies within the diftance of a fummer-evening walk, bring together fuch a variety of uncommon, and beautiful circumftances, as are rarely to be found in one place.

Very little had been done, at Ilam, when we faw it, to embellifh it's natural fituation; tho it is capable of great improvement; particularly in the front of the houfe. There the ground, which is now a formal flowergarden, might eafily be united with the other parts of the fcenery in it's neighbourhood. It is now totally at variance with it.

In the higher part of the garden, under a rock, is a feat dedicated to the memory of Congreve; where, we were told by our conductor, he compofed feveral of his plays.

From

From Ilam we went to Oakover to fee the *holy family* by Raphael. As this picture is very celebrated, we gave it a minute examination.

Whether it be an original, I am not critic enough in the works of Raphael to determine. I fhould fuppofe, it is; and it were a pity to rob it of it's greateft merit. Nothing, I think, but the character of the mafter could give it the reputation it holds. If it be examined by the rules of painting, it is certainly deficient. The manner is hard, without freedom; and the colouring black, without fweetnefs. Neither is there any harmony in the whole. What harmony can arife from a conjunction of red, blue, and yellow, of which the draperies are compofed, almoft in raw tints? Nor is the deficiency in the colouring, compenfated by any harmony in the light and fhade.

But thefe things perhaps we are not led to expect in the works of Raphael. In them we feek for grace, drawing, character, and expreffion. Here however they are not found. The virgin, we allow to be a lovely figure:

Q 4

but

but Joſeph is inanimate; the boys are grin-
ning ſatyrins; and with regard to drawing,
the right arm of Chriſt, I ſhould ſuppoſe, is
very faulty.*

On the whole, a holy family is a ſubject
but indifferently adapted to the pencil. Unleſs the painter could give the mother that
celeſtial love; and the child, that *divine com-
poſure*, and *ſweetneſs*, (which, I take it for
granted, no painter can give,) the ſubject
immediately degenerates into *a mother*, and *a
child*. The *actions* of our Saviour's life may
be good ſubjects for a picture: for altho the
divine energy of the principal figure cannot
be expreſſed; yet the other parts of the ſtory
being well told, may ſupply that deficiency.
But in a holy family there is *no action*—no
ſtory told—the whole conſiſts in the expreſ-
ſion of characters and affections, which we

---

* Since I made theſe remarks I was glad to ſee a kind
of ſanction given them by a great authority. Sir Joſhua
Reynolds, in one of his lectures, before the academy,
ſpeaks very ſlightly of the *eaſel-pictures* of Raphael; which,
he ſays, give us no idea of that great maſter's genius.

muſt

muſt ſuppoſe beyond conception. So that if theſe are not expreſſed, the whole is nothing.

In the ſame room hang three or four pictures, any of which I ſhould value more than the celebrated *Raphael*. There is a ſmall picture, by Rubens, repreſenting the angels appearing to the women in the garden, which pleaſed me. The angels indeed are clumſey figures; and dreſſed like choiriſters: but every other part of the picture, and the management of the whole, is good.

In a large picture alſo of the unjuſt ſteward, the family in diſtreſs is well deſcribed: but on the whole, it is one of thoſe ambiguous pictures, on which we cannot well pronounce *at ſight*. One half of it ſeems painted by *Rubens*; of the other half we doubted.

There are alſo in the ſame room two very capital *Vanderveldts*—a calm, and a ſtorm. Both are good: but the former pleaſed me better, than almoſt any picture by that maſter, I have any where ſeen.

SECT.

S E C T. XXX.

FROM Aſhburn, to which we returned from Oakover, we went, the next day, through a chearful, woody country, to Keddleſton, the ſeat of lord Scarſdale.

The ſituation of Keddleſton, participates little of the romantic country, on which it borders. The houſe ſtands in a pleaſant park, rather bare of wood; but the deficiency is in a great degree compenſated by the beauty of the trees; ſome of which are large, and noble. A ſtream, by the help of art, is changed into a river, over which you are conducted by a good approach obliquely to the houſe.

The architecture of Keddleſton, as far as I could judge, is a compoſition of elegance, and grandeur. The main body of the houſe, which you enter by a noble portico, is joined, by a corridore on each ſide, to a handſome wing.

wing. In the back front, the saloon, which
is a rotunda, appears to advantage. From the
hall lead the state rooms, which are not many.
The rest of the house consists of excellent
offices, and comfortable apartments; and the
plan of the whole is easy, and intelligible.

The hall is perhaps one of the grandest,
and most beautiful private rooms in England.
The roof is supported by very noble columns;
some of which are intire blocks of marble,
dug, as we were informed, from lord Scars-
dale's own quarries. It is rather indeed a
spurious sort of marble; but more beautiful,
at least in colour, than any that is imported.
There is a richness, and a variety in it, that
pleases the eye exceedingly: the veins are
large, and suited to columns; and a rough
polish, *by receiving the light in one body*, gives
a noble swell to the column; and adds much
to it's beauty.

When I saw this grand room, I thought it
wanted no farther decoration. All was simple,
great, and uniform, as it ought to be. Since
that time I have heard the doors, and windows
have been painted, and varnished in the cabinet
style. I have not seen these alterations; and
cannot pronounce on their merit: but I am

at

at a lofs to conceive, that any farther embellifhment could add to the effect.

The *entrance* of a great houfe, fhould, in
my opinion, confift only of that kind of beauty,
which arifes merely from fimplicity and grandeur. Thefe ideas, as you proceed in the apartments, may detail themfelves into ornaments
of various kinds; and, in their *proper places*,
even into prettineffes. Alien, mifplaced, am-
bitious ornaments, no doubt, are *every where*
difgufting: but in the *grand entrance* of a
houfe, they fhould *particularly* be avoided. A
falfe tafte, difcovered there, is apt to purfue
you through the apartments; and throw it's
colours on what may happen to be good.—I
fhould be unwilling however to fuppofe, that
any improper decorations are added to the hall
at Keddlefton; as the ornaments of the houfe,
in general, when I faw it, feemed to be under
the conduct of a chaft and elegant tafte. Tho
every thing was rich; I do not recollect, that
any thing was tawdry, trifling, or affected.

The pictures, of which there is a confiderable collection, are chiefly, what may be called
good *furniture pictures.** A Rembrandt is

---

* See page 24, Vol. I.

the

the firſt in rank; and is indeed a valuable piece. It repreſents *Daniel interpreting Belteſhazzar's dream*. There is great amuſement in this picture. It is highly finiſhed; and the heads are particularly excellent. For the reſt, it is a ſcattered piece, without any idea of compoſition.

In the drawing-room are two large uprights by Benedetto Lutti; one repreſenting the laſt ſupper; the other the death of Abel. They are painted in a ſingular manner with ſtrong lights. The former has a good effect. The death of Abel is likewiſe a ſhewy picture; but has nothing very ſtriking in it, except the figure of Cain.

In the dead game by Snyders, there is a good fawn; but the picture is made diſagreeable by the *glaring* tail of a peacock.

In the dead game and dogs, by Fyt, there are good *paſſages*, but no *whole*.

The *woman of Samaria*, and *St. John in the wilderneſs*, by B. Stiozzi, are good pictures.

There is alſo a large Coyp, well-painted; but badly compoſed.

At

At Derby, which lies within three miles of Keddlefton, we were immediatly ftruck with the tower of the great church, which is a beautiful piece of Gothic architecture.

The object of the china-works there is merely ornament; which is particularly unhappy, as they were, at the time we faw them, under no regulation of tafte. A very free hand we found employed in painting the vafes; and the firft colours were *laid in* with fpirit: but in the *finifhing*, they were fo richly daubed, that all freedom was loft in finery.—It may now be otherwife.

The gaudy painters however of fuch works, have the example of a great mafter before them. even Raphael himfelf; whofe paintings in the pottery way, tho highly efteemed in the cabinets of the curious, feem generally to be daubed with very glaring colours. It is faid, that Raphael fell in love with a potter's daughter; and that to pleafe her, he painted her father's difhes.

difhes. It is probable therefore, that he fuited them to her tafte; which accounts for the gaudy colouring they difplay.—How much more fimple, elegant, and beautiful is the painting of the old Etrufcan vafes, many of which Mr. Wedgewood has fo happily imitated? There we fee how much better an effect is produced by chaft colours on a dark ground; than by gaudy colours, on a light one.

A perfon curious in machinery would be much amufed by the filk-mill at Derby, in which thirty thoufand little wheels are put in motion by one great wheel. The various parts, tho fo complicated in appearance, are yet fo diftinct in their movements; that we were told, any one workman has the power of ftopping that part of the machinery, which is under his direction, without interrupting the motion of the reft.

The country between Derby and Leicefter is flat. Quardon-wood, a little beyond Loughborough, rifing on the right, makes an agreeable variety, amidft fuch a continuation of uniformity.

uniformity. Mount Sorrel alfo has the fame
effect.

The approach to Leicefter gives it more confequence than it really has. The town itfelf,
old and incumbered, has little beauty: but
it abounds with fragments of antiquity.

Behind St. Nicholas's church is a piece of
Roman architecture; one of the only *pure*
pieces perhaps in England. We fee many
towers, which go by the name of Cæfar; and
boaft of Roman origin. I doubt, whether
any of them can boaft it with truth. And
what few *remnants* we have, it is thought,
have all been retouched in after times. This
fragment feems to have fuffered no alteration.
It's infignificance has fecured it. Little more
is left, than a wall, with four double arches
on it's face, retiring, but not perforated. And
yet in this trifling remnant there is a fimplicity
and dignity, which are very pleafing. It is
poffible however that prejudice may in part,
be the fource of it's beauty. Through an affo-

ciation of ideas, we may here be pleafed with what we have admired in Italian views.— This wall is built of brick; tho it has probably been faced with better materials. For what purpofe it was conftructed, does not appear: nor whether it was intended for the end, or fide of a building. The idea of the country is, that it has been a temple, from the great number of bones of animals, which have been found near it: from whence it takes the name of *Holy-bones*.

The church of St. Nicholas, which ftands oppofite to it, feems to have been built out of it's ruins, from the many Roman bricks with which it abounds. Indeed the ftyle of building, in the body of the church, is not unlike it.

At Leicefter alfo we were put on the purfuit of another Roman fragment—a curious piece of fculpture; which we found at laft in a cellar. It is a fcrap of teffulated pavement, on which three figures are reprefented; a ftag; a woman leaning over it; and a boy fhooting

with

with a bow. It may be a piece of Roman antiquity; but it is a piece of miserable work-manship.

In this ancient town are found also many vestiges of British antiquity.—From so rich an endowment as the abbey of Leicester formerly possessed, we expected many beautiful remains; as it is still in a kind of sequestered state : but in that expectation we were disappointed. Not the least fragment of a Gothic window is left: not the merest mutilation of an arch. It's present remains afford as little beauty, as the ruins of a common dwelling. And in all probability the present ruin has only been a common dwelling; built from the materials of the ancient abbey. Such at least is the tradition of the place. It belonged formerly, we were told, to the family of Haftings; and was loft at play to the earl of Devonfhire : but before the conveyance was prepared; the owner, in the fpirit of revenge, and mortification, fent private orders to have it burnt.—Many a black tale might be unfolded in old houfes, if walls could fpeak.

But

But the great ftory of this abbey has a vir-
tuous tendency. Within it's walls was once
exhibited a fcene more humiliating to human
ambition, and more inftructive to human
grandeur, than almoft any, which hiftory hath
produced. Here the fallen pride of Woolfey
retreated from the infults of the world. All
his vifions of ambition were now gone; his
pomp; and pageantry; and crouded levees.
On this fpot he told the liftening monks, the
fole attendants of his dying hour, as they ftood
around his pallet, that he was come to lay his
bones among them: and gave that pathetic
teftimony to the truth, and joys of religion,
which preaches beyond a thoufand lectures.
" If I had ferved God as faithfully as I ferved
the king, he would not thus have forfaken
my old age."

The death of Woolfey would make a fine
moral picture; if the hand of any mafter could
give the pallid features of the dying ftatefman
that chagrin, that remorfe, thofe pangs of
anguifh, which, in thefe laft bitter moments
of his life, poffeffed him.——The point might
be taken, when the monks are adminiftring
the

the comforts of religion, which the defpair-
ing prelate cannot feel. The fubject requires
a gloomy apartment; which a ray through a
Gothic window might juft enlighten; throw-
ing it's force chiefly on the principal figure;
and dying away on the reft. The appendages
of the piece need only be few, and fimple;
little more than the crozier, and red hat, to
mark the cardinal, and tell the ftory.

This is not the only piece of Englifh hiftory,
which is illuftrated in this ancient town.——
Here the houfe is ftill fhewn, where Richard
III. paffed the night, before the battle of Bof-
worth: and there is a ftory of him, ftill
preferved in the *corporation-records*, as we
were informed by our conductor, (who did
not however appear to be a man of deep eru-
dition) which illuftrates the caution and darknefs of that prince's character.——It was his
cuftom to carry, among the baggage of his
camp, a cumberfome, wooden bed, which he
pretended was the only bed he could fleep in.
Here he contrived a fecret receptacle for his
treafure, which lay concealed under a weight
of timber. After the fatal day, on which

R 3 Richard

Richard fell, the earl of Richmond entered
Leicester with his victorious troops. The
friends of Richard were pillaged; but the bed
was neglected by every plunderer, as useless
lumber.—The owner of the house afterwards
discovering the hoard, became suddenly rich,
without any visible cause. He bought lands;
and at length (as our intelligencer informed
us) arrived at the dignity of being mayor of
Leicester. Many years afterwards, his widow,
who had been left in great affluence, was
murdered for her wealth by a servant maid,
who had been privy to the affair: and at the
trial of this woman, and her accomplices, the
whole transaction came to light.

S E C T. XXXI.

FROM Leicefter the country ftill continues flat and woody; ftretching out into
meadows, paftures, and common fields. The
horizon, on every fide, is generally terminated
by fpires. Oftener than once we were able
to count fix, or feven adorning the limits of
one circular view.

Of all the countries in England, this is the
place for that noble fpecies of diverfion, to
which the inventive genius of our young fportf-
men hath given the name of *fteeple-hunting*.
In a dearth of game, the chaffeurs draw up
in a body, and pointing to fome confpicuous
fteeple, fet off, in full fpeed towards it, over
hedge and ditch. He who is fo happy, as to
arrive firft, receives equal honour, it is faid,

R 4   as

as if he had come in foremoft, at the death
of the fox.

In thefe plains, as rich, as they are unpicturefque, we had nothing to obferve, but the
numerous herds of cattle, and flocks of fheep,
which graze them: and in the deficiency of
other objects, we amufed ourfelves with the
various forms of thefe animals, and their moft
agreeable combinations.

The horfe in itfelf, is certainly a nobler
animal, than the cow. His form is more
elegant; and his fpirit gives fire and grace to
his actions. But in a *picturefque light* the
cow has undoubtedly the advantage; and is
every way better fuited to receive the graces
of the pencil.

In the firft place, the lines of the horfe
are round and fmooth; and admit little variety: whereas the bones of the cow are high,
and vary the line, here and there, by a fquare-
nefs, which is very picturefque. There is a
greater proportion alfo of concavity in them;
the lines of the horfe being chiefly convex.

But

But is not the lean, worn-out horfe, whofe bones are ftaring, as picturefque as the cow? In a degree it is; but we do not with pleafure admit the idea of beauty into any deficient form. Prejudice, even in fpite of us, rather revolts againft fuch an admiffion, however picturefque.

The cow alfo has the advantage, not only in it's picturefque lines; but in the mode of filling them up. If the horfe be fleek efpecially, and have, what the jockies call, a *fine coat*, the fmoothnefs of the furface is not fo well adapted to receive the fpirited touches of the pencil, as the rougher form and coat of the cow. The very action of licking herfelf, which is fo common among cows, throws the hair, when it is long, into different feathery flakes; and gives it thofe ftrong touches, which are indeed the very touches of the pencil.—Cows are commonly the moft picturefque in the months of April, and May, when the old hair is coming off. There is a contraft between the rougher, and fmoother parts of the coat; and often alfo a pleafing variety of greyifh tints, blended with others of a richer hue. We obferve this too

in

in colts, when we fee them in a ftate of nature.

The cow is better adapted alfo to receive the beauties of light. The horfe, like a piece of fmooth garden-ground, receives it in a gradual fpread: the cow, like the abruptnefs of a rugged country, receives it in bold catches. And tho in *large objects* a *gradation* of light is one great fource of beauty; yet, in a *fmall object*, it has not commonly fo pleafing an effect, as arifes from *fmart, catching lights*.

The *colour* of the cow alfo is often more picturefque. That of the horfe is generally uniform. Whereas the tints of the cow frequently play into each other; a dark head melting into lighter fides; and thefe again being ftill darker than the hinder parts. Thofe are always the moft beautiful, which are thus tinted with dark colours, harmonioufly ftealing into lighter. Here and there a few fmall white fpots may add a beauty; but if they run into large blotches, and make a harfh termination between the dark, and light colour, they are difagreeable. The full black alfo, and full red, have little variety in *themfelves*; tho in a *group* all this unpleafant colouring may harmonize.

In

In the *character*, and *general form* of cows, as well as of horfes, there are many degrees of beauty and deformity.

The *character* of the cow is marked chiefly in the head. An open, or contracted forehead; a long or a fhort vifage; the twift of a horn; or the colour of an eyebrow; will totally alter the *character*, and give a four, or an agreeable air to the countenance. Nor is the head of this animal more characteriftic, than it is adapted to receive the graces of the pencil.

With regard to the *general form* of the cow, we are not indeed fo exact, as in that of the horfe. The points and proportions of the horfe are ftudied, and determined with fo much exactnefs, that a fmall deviation ftrikes the eye. In the form of the cow, we are not fo learned. If *deformity* be avoided, it is enough. There are two faults particularly in the line of a cow, a *hog-back*, and a *finking rump*, which are it's moft ufual blemifhes. If it be free from thefe, and have an harmonious colouring, and a pleafant character, it cannot well be difagreeable.

The

The *bull* and the *cow* differ more in *character* and *form*, than the horfe and the mare. They are caft in *different moulds*. The fournefs of the head; the thicknefs and convexity of the neck; the heavinefs of the cheft, and fhoulders; the fmoothnefs of the hip-bones; and the lightnefs of the hind-quarters, are always found in the bull; and rarely in the cow.

The fheep is as beautiful an animal, as the cow; and as well adapted to receive the graces of painting. Tho it want the variety of colouring; yet there is a foftnefs in it's fleece, a richnefs, a delicacy of touch, and a fweet tendernefs of fhadow, which make it a very pleafing object.

The fheep is beautiful in every ftate, except juft when it has paft under the fheers. But it foon recovers it's beauty; and in a few weeks lofes it's furrowed fides, and appears again in a picturefque drefs. It's beauty continues, as the wool increafes. What it lofes in fhape, it gains in the feathered flakinefs of it's fleece. Nor is it the leaft beautiful, when it's fides are a little ragged— when part of it's fhape is difcovered, and

part

part hid beneath the wool. Berghem de-. lights to reprefent it in this ragged form.

In the *characters*, and *forms* of fheep we obferve little difference. We fometimes fee an unpleafing vifage; and fometimes the dif- agreeable rounding line, which we have juft called the hog-back: but in an animal fo fmall, the eye is lefs apt to inveftigate *parts*: it rather refts on the *whole appearance*; and the more fo, as fheep being particularly gre- garious, are generally confidered as objects in a group.

The obfervations I have made with regard to the beauty of thefe animals, are confirmed by the practice of all the great mafters in ani- mal life, Berghem, Coyp, Potter and others; who always preferred them to horfes and deer, in adorning their rural fcenes.—It is an ad- ditional pleafure therefore, that fuch animals, as are the moft ufeful, are likewife the moft ornamental.

Having thus examined the *forms* of thefe picturefque animals, we fpent fome time alfo

in

in examining their moſt agreeable *combinations*.

Cattle are ſo large, that when they ornament a foreground, a few are ſufficient. Two cows will hardly combine. Three make a good group—either united—or when one is a little removed from the other two. If you increaſe the group beyond three; one, or more, in proportion, muſt neceſſarily be a *little detached*. This detachment prevents heavineſs, and adds variety. It is the ſame principle applied to cattle, which we before applied to mountains, and other objeɛts.*

The ſame rules in grouping may be applied to *diſtant cattle*; only here you may introduce a greater number.

In grouping, contraſted attitudes ſhould be ſtudied. Recumbency ſhould be oppoſed to a ſtanding poſture; foreſhortened figures, to lengthened; and one colour, to another. White blotches may enliven a group, tho in a ſingle animal, we obſerved, they are offenſive.

---

* See page 55, Vol. II. &c.

Sheep

Sheep come under the same rules; only the *foreground*, as well as the *diftance*, admits a larger number of thefe fmaller animals. In paftoral fubjects fheep are often ornamental, when *dotted about* the fides of *diftant* hills. Here little more is neceffary, than to guard againft regular fhapes—lines; circles; and croffes; which large flocks of fheep fometimes form. In combining them however, or, rather fcattering them, the painter may keep in view the principle, we have already fo often inculcated. They may be huddled together, in one, or more large bodies; from which little groups of different fizes, in proportion to the larger, fhould be detached.

In favour of the doctrine I have here advanced of the *fubordinate group*, I cannot forbear adding the authority of a great mafter, whofe thorough acquaintance with every part of painting hath often, in the courfe of this work, been obferved.

Æneas, landing on the coaft of Africa, fees from the higher ground a herd of deer feeding in a valley; and Virgil, who, in the flighteft inftance, feems ever to have had before his eyes, ideas of picturefque beauty, introduces

introduces the herd, juſt as a painter would have done. From the *larger group* he detaches a *ſubordinate one* :

> ——————————*Tres* litore cervos
> Proſpicit errantes; hos *tota armenta* ſequuntur
> A tergo,——————————

I need not conceal, that ſome commentators have found in theſe three ſtags, which the herd followed, the poet's inclination to ariſtocracy; and that others have ſuppoſed, he meant a compliment to the triumvirate. It is the commentator's buſineſs to find out a recondite meaning : common ſenſe is ſatisfied with what is moſt obvious.

It may be obſerved further, that *cattle* and *ſheep* mix very agreeably *together*; as alſo *young* animals, and *old*. Lambs and calves fill up little interſtices in a group, and aſſiſt the combination.—I may add, that *human figures* alſo combine very agreeably with *animals*. Indeed they generally give a grace to a group, as they draw it to an *apex*.

I need

I need not apologize for this long digreſſion, as it is ſo naturally ſuggeſted by the country, through which we paſſed ; and ſo cloſely connected with the ſubject, which we treat. He who ſtudies landſcape, will find himſelf very deficient, if he hath not paid great attention to the choice, and combination, both of animal and human figures.

S E C T. XXXII.

LEAVING the plains of Leicesterfhire, we entered the county of Northampton, which affumes a new face. The ground begins to rife and fall, and diftances to open.

Lord Strafford's gardens, extending a confiderable way on the left, are a great ornament to the country.

Lord Hallifax's improvements fucceed. They make little appearance from the road : but the road itfelf is fo beautiful, that it requires no aid. It paffes through fpacious lanes, adorned on each fide by a broad, irregular border of grafs ; and winds through hedge-rows of full-grown oak, which the feveral turns of the

S 2

road

road form into clumps. You have both a good fore ground, and beautiful views into a fine country, through the boles of the trees. The undreffed fimplicity, and native beauty, of fuch lanes as thefe, exceed the walks of the moft finifhed garden.

From Newport-Pagnel the country ftill continues pleafant. Before we reach Wooburn, we have a good view of Wooburn-abbey, and of the furrounding woods; which decorate the landfcape.

Wooburn-park is an extenfive woody fcene, and capable of much improvement. We rode through it: but could not fee the duke of Bedford's houfe; which is fhewn only on particular days,—But the difappointment was not great. The *furniture* of all fine houfes is much the fame; and as for pictures (fuch is the prevalence of *names*, and fafhion) that fometimes what are called the beft collections, fcarce repay the ceremonies you are obliged to go through in getting a fight of them.

After

‹ After we leave Wooburn, the views continue ſtill pleaſant; till we meet the chalky
hills of Dunſtable. Theſe would. disfigure
the lovelieſt ſcene. But when we have paſſed
theſe glaring heights, the country revives:
the riſing grounds are covered with wood,
and verdure; and the whole looks pleaſing.
About Redburn particularly the country is
beautiful; and is thrown into diſtance by
large oaks, which over-hang the road.

St. Albans' church, and the ruins about
it, make an immenſe pile; of which ſome parts
are piƈtureſque. There is a mixture too of
brick and ſtone in the building, which often
makes a pleaſing contraſt in the tints. Tho
there are many remains of beautiful Gothic
in this church; there are more deformities
of Saxon architeƈture; particularly the tower,
which is heavy, and diſagreeably ornamented.
The little ſpire, which ariſes from it, is very
abſurd.——Within the church is a monument
near the altar, of very curious Gothic work-
manſhip.

Among

Among the numerous inhabitants of the fubterraneous regions of this church, lies that celebrated prince, remembered by the name of good duke Humphrey; the youngeft brother of Henry V. He was put to death by a faction, in the fucceeding reign; and was buried fomewhere in this abbey; but his grave was unknown. Having lain concealed near three centuries, he came again to light, not many years ago. By an accident, a large vault was difcovered, in which he was found fole tenant; wrapped in lead, and immerfed in a pickle, which had preferved him in tolerable order.

Near St. Albans ftood the city of Verulam; formerly one of the greateft feats of the Roman empire in Britain. It was facked, and deftroyed by Boadicia, when that heroine, exafperated againft the Romans, cut in pieces their armies. Camden carries the dignity of it into times ftill more remote; and fuppofes it to have been that foreft-town, where Caffibelin defended himfelf againft Cæfar.

Beyond

Beyond Verulam the country grows pleafant.
From Barnet, the road enters Finchley-com-
mon. The diftance is woody, interfected by
an extenfive plain, which is connected with
it by a fprinkling of fcattered trees. The
parts are large; and the fcenery not unpicturefque.

The firft view of Highgate-hill would make
a good diftance, if it were properly fupported
by a fore-ground. The view *from* it, is very
grand; but is diftracted by a multiplicity of
objects.

After this the country is gone. London
comes on apace; and all thofe difgufting ideas,
with which it's great avenues abound—brick-
kilns fteaming with offenfive fmoke—fewers
and ditches fweating with filth—heaps of collected foil, and ftinks of every denomination—
clouds of duft, rifing and vanifhing, from agi-
tated wheels, purfuing each other in rapid
motion—or taking ftationary poffeffion of the
road,

road, by becoming the atmofphere of fome cumberfome, flow-moving waggon—villages without rural ideas—trees, and hedge-rows without a tinge of green—and fields and mea-dows without pafturage; in which lowing bullocks are crouded together, waiting for the fhambles; or cows penned, like hogs, to feed on grains.—It was an agreeable relief to get through this fucceffion of noifome objects, which did violence to all the fenfes by turns: and to leave behind us *the bufy hum of men*; ftealing from it through the quiet lanes of Sur-ry; which leading to no great mart, or general rendezvous, afford calmer retreats on every fide, than can eafily be found in the neighbourhood of fo great a town.

July 3, 1772.

T H E   E N D.

EXPLANATION

OF THE

PRINTS.

V O L U M E I.

P A G E 38.

A VIEW of Warwick-caſtle, from the park; in which it's connection with the river, and iſland are repreſented.

P A G E 76.

A ſpecimen of the elegant mode, in which handles are adapted to Tuſcan vaſes; and the awkward manner in which they are commonly affixed to thoſe of modern conſtruction.

a

PAGE

P A G E 90.

An explanation of the ſhapes and lines of mountains. They are left unſhadowed, that their forms may be more conſpicuous,

P A G E 102.

An illuſtration of the appearance, which the ſhores of a lake form, when ſeen *from it's ſurface, in a boat.* The promontories, and bays, unleſs very large, loſe all their indentations; and the whole boundary of the lake becomes a mere thread.

When you ſtand *upon the ſhore,* if your ſituation be, in any degree, elevated, the promontories appear to come forward; and all the indentations are diſtinct.

Theſe two modes of viewing may be compared by turning from this print to page 55, vol. II; in which is repreſented a lake ſeen *from the ſhore.* This latter mode of viewing a lake is generally the moſt pleaſing; unleſs
indeed

indeed the ſtand be taken too high, which elevates the horizon too much.

P A G E 106.

This print is meant to exemplify thoſe beautiful reflections, which are ſometimes formed on the ſurface of a lake; and broken by it's tremulous motion; as explained in page 107.

P A G E 120.

The *contracted valley* may be conſidered as a ſpecies of foreground. Theſe ſcenes are generally decorated with a river; but ſometimes only with a road. Of this latter kind is Middleton-dale, deſcribed in the 209th page of the IId vol.

The *contracted valley* is contraſted by the open, *extended vale*; a ſcene of which kind is repreſented in the 41ſt page of the IId vol.

P A G E 131.

An illuſtration of the *effect of light* ; which is ſo great, as to give conſequence even where there are no objects. A ſetting ſun ; or a ſtorm, (as here repreſented) are moſt favourable to an exhibition of this kind.

P A G E 142.

This plan of Windermere is not geographically exact ; but enough ſo to give the reader an idea of it's ſhape, and the ſituation of the ſeveral places mentioned on it's ſhores.

P A G E 143.

This view of the middle part of Windermere, is taken from the grounds a little to the north of Bowneſs. The diſtance, as the reader will obſerve from the plan, is compoſed of that country, which ſhoots away towards the ſouth. The high grounds make a

part

part of Furnefs-fell; which is defcribed, in page 151, ftretching along the weftern fhores of the lake towards the north.—Below Fur-nefs-fell appear fome of the iflands of the lake, particularly the great ifland; which is the moft fouthern of them.

PAGE 165.

This is a view of that part of Furnefs-abbey, which is called the *fchool*; and which is one of the moft beautiful fragments of that elegant ruin. I had this very pleafing drawing from Mr. Smith.

PAGE 171.

An illuftration of that kind of wild country, of which we faw feveral inftances, as we en-tered Cumberland. In general, the mountains make the moft confiderable part of thefe fcenes. But when any of them is furnifhed with a diftant view of a lake, the landfcape is greatly inriched.

PAGE

P A G E 187.

This plan of Kefwick-lake means only to exprefs the general fhape of it; and the relative fituation of it's feveral parts.

P A G E 195.

The character of that fort of rocky fcenery is here given, which is not uncommonly found on the banks of lakes, particularly of Kefwick lake; the fhores of which exhibit feveral inftances of thefe detached rocks.

P A G E 201.

An illuftration of that fort of country, which compofes the narrower parts of the ftraits of Borrodale. They confift of rocky, or craggy mountains on each fide; with a ftream, or, in fome parts, (where the ftream may be hid) a road in the middle. But it is difficult to give any idea of thefe tremendous fcenes, in fo fmall a compafs, as they are here exhibited: for as

their

their terror confifts greatly in their immenfity, it is not eafy to perfuade the eye to conceive highly of their grandeur from thefe diminutive reprefentations.—Mr. Farrington has given us, on a larger fcale, a fine portrait, and I think, a very exact one, of the entrance into thefe ftraits at the village of Grange.

P A G E 235.

This print was intended to give fome idea of that kind of rocky fcenery, of which Gates-garth-dale is compofed. The clouds fweeping over the fummits of the rocks, which were reprefented in the firft edition, are left out here; as I found they could not eafily be expreffed.

VOLUME II.

P A G E 41.

AN illuftration of that beautiful fpecies of landfcape, produced by an *extenfive vale*. Gradation is among the firft principles of picturefque beauty. A graduating light, a graduating fhade, or a graduating diftance, are all beautiful. When the vale therefore does not exceed fuch a proportion, as is adapted to the eye, it is pleafing to fee it fading away gradually, from the foreground, into the obfcurity of diftance. It prefents indeed only *one uniform* idea; which, tho often *grand*, is not generally fo *pleafing*, as the variety, and intricacy of a country broken into parts, and yet harmonioufly combined.

P A G E 51.

This plan of Ullefwater, like the others, is not very exact; but enough fo, to give an idea of it's general fhape, and the relative fituation of the feveral places on it's fhores.

P A G E 55.

This print illuftrates that kind of fcenery, which is prefented by Ullefwater. It is, by no means, a portrait: but it gives fome idea of the view towards Patterdale, in which the rocky promontory on the left, and the two woody promontories on the right, are confpicuous features.

P A G E 85.

This view has more the air of Dacre-caftle than of any of the other old caftles we met with: but it is chiefly introduced to fhew the beautiful effect which fome of thefe ruins had, when feen, under a gloomy hemifphere, inlightened by the rays of a fetting fun.

PAGE

PAGE 121.

A view of Scaleby-castle, in which the old tower part of the walls, and the bastion, are reprefented.

PAGE 169.

An illuftration of the force of contraft, in a piece of regular ground, bifected.

PAGE 221.

This print is meant to give fome idea of that kind of continuation of rocky fcenery, which is found at Matlock, along the banks of the Derwent.

PAGE 227.

This view of *Dove-dale*, reprefents that beautiful fcene in a more naked ftate, than it is defcribed. The bare rock only is here reprefented; which the fpectator's imagination muft cloath with wood, to give it compleat beauty.

beauty.—The fact is, a little gain unluckily arises from difmantling it periodically of it's wood; and this drawing was made, juft after the axe had been at work.

P A G E 247.

An illuftration of that kind of *flat country* which we meet with in Leicefterfhire. The horizon is generally bounded by a diftance, and yet feldom an extenfive one; as there is rarely a rifing ground, that can command it. The country is uninterefting, and wants adventitious objects to fet it off. If the diftance happen to be fpread with light under a dark cloud, it is a happy circumftance; and has a good effect. Sometimes, on the middle grounds, a gentle rife, adorned with a fpire; or a fhepherd attending his flock, may relieve the eye. Such circumftances are all we can expect. In defect of thefe, we muft be fatisfied with a few cattle on the foreground, which may turn the *landfcape* into an *appendage*; and give us one of the pictures of Coyp.

PAGE

P A G E 249:

This print exhibits a comparifon between the lines of the horfe and the cow, as objects of picturefque beauty.

P A G E 252.

This exhibits the fame mode of comparifon between the bull, and the cow.

P A G E 254.

Thefe two prints are meant to explain the doctrine of grouping *larger cattle*. *Two* will hardly combine. There is indeed no way of forming *two* into a group, but by *uniting* them, as they are reprefented in the former of thefe prints. If they ftand apart, whatever their attitudes, or fituation may be, there will be a deficiency.

But with *three*, you are almoft fure of a good group, except indeed they all ftand in the fame attitude, and at equal diftances. They generally however combine the moft beautifully, when two are *united*, and the third a little *removed*.

Four introduce a new difficulty in grouping. *Separate* they would have a bad effect. Two,

and

and two together would be equally bad. The only way, in which they will group well, is to *unite three,* as reprefented in the fecond of thefe prints, and to *remove the fourth.*

P A G E 255.

Thefe two prints illuftrate the doctrine of grouping *fmaller animals,* as fheep, goats, and deer. When they occupy the *foreground,* as reprefented in the firft, they come under the fame rule of grouping, as larger cattle: only a greater number may be introduced. And if the main body be larger, the fubordinate group muft be fo of courfe.

If they be removed to a *middle diftance,* as reprefented in the other of thefe prints, the fubordinate group is of lefs confequence; and ftill of lefs, the farther it recedes from the eye. The whole is only confidered as one body, blended, as it were, and fhadowed, or inlightened with the ground: and it is enough, if regular, and difagreeable fhapes are avoided.

ERRATA.

VOL. I.

For *only family seat*, read *old family seat*, page 22.
For *in one scene by the trees*, read *in one scene with the lawn, which is the foreground, by the trees*, p. 42.
For *kind of red brick*, read *kind of brick*, p. 57.
For *origion of the lake*, read *origin of the lake*, p. 100.
For *painted after*, read *panted after*. p. 123.
For *shifting to his beam* read *shifting to his beam*. p. 184.

VOL. II.

For *Skiddaw.—Threlkate*, read *Skiddaw——Threlkate*, p. 39.
For *still remembred*, read *still remembred)* p. 124.
For *fluttered with rags* read *fluttering with rags*. p. 125.
For *overflowing from the* read *from the overflowing of*. p. 133.
For *pieces of scenery* read *scenes*. p. 227.

Published by the same Author.

Lives of several Reformers.

Lectures on the church-catechism, for the use of schools. Price 2s.

An Exposition of the New Testament, pointing out the *leading sense*, and *connection* of the sacred writers.

Two sermons, On *comparing spiritual things with spiritual.*—— And on the *Simplicity of the gospel.*

An Essay on Prints.

Picturesque remarks on the river Wye.

————————— the Highlands of Scotland.

————————— Forest-scenery.

Three Essays—on picturesque beauty——on picturesque travel ——and on the art of sketching landscape.

Life of John Trueman, &c. for the use of kitchens, cottages, and farm-houses; price ten-pence, or 26 copies for £1. or 108 for £4.

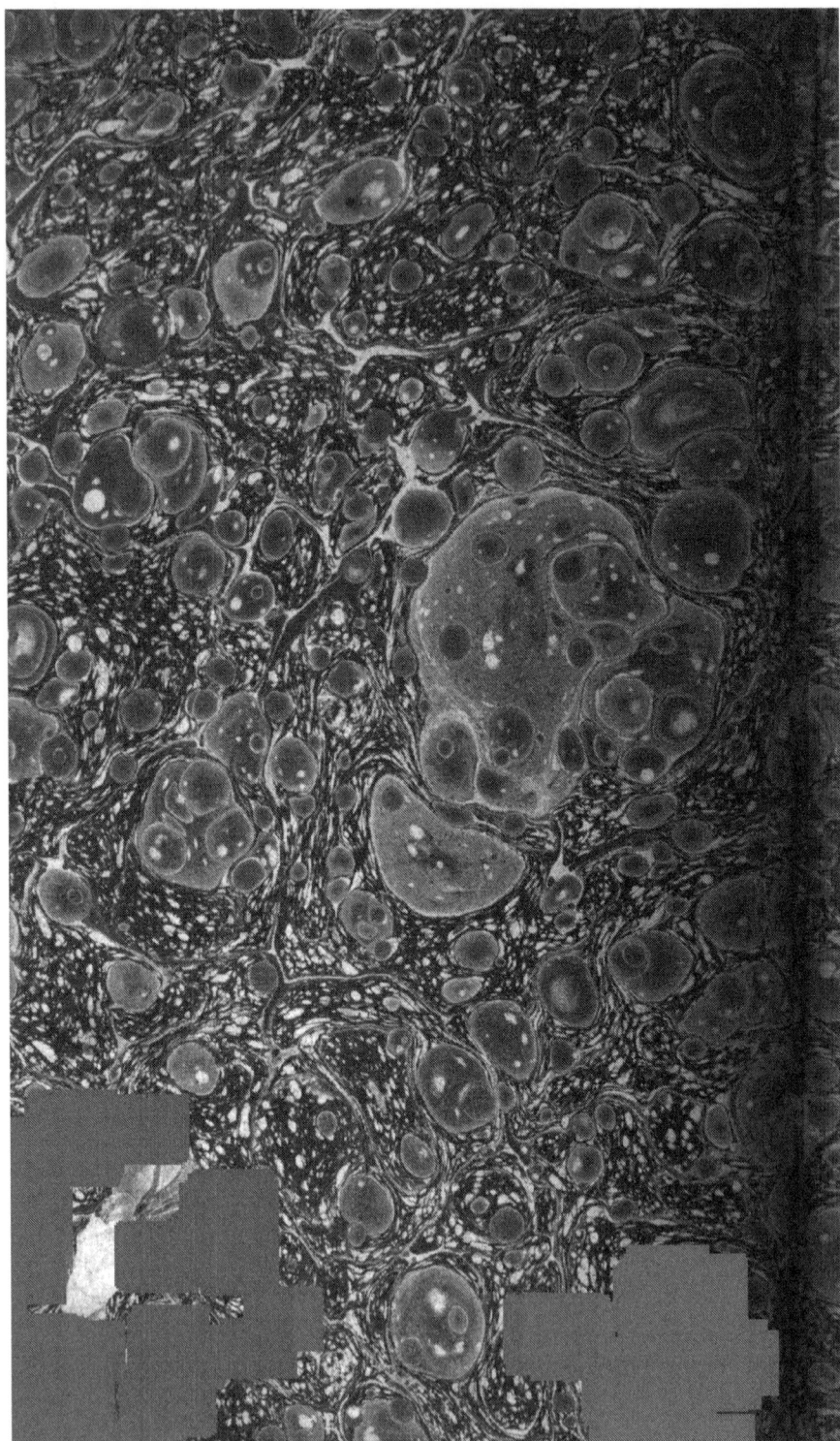

Lightning Source UK Ltd.
Milton Keynes UK
UKHW020716311221
396440UK00006B/450